"Are you really offering me a job, Rogan?" Carolina asked. "And where do you expect me to live?" she said.

"Right here, Goldilocks. Right here with me," Sean Rogan said.

"Oh, Rogan, thank you." Impulsively she slid across the seat, tucked an errant strand of hair behind his ear, and planted a kiss on his cheek. "I very much want to be here with you."

Rogan gulped in a breath of air, parked the truck, and pulled her into his arms with a growl of frustration. He'd fought the urge all day and he couldn't stop himself any longer. He wanted to hold her, nothing more.

She stiffened for a moment, then melted against him.

"You know this was all your idea," he whispered, his face pressed against her hair.

"I expected you to push me away," she said softly.

"Does this look like I'm pushing?" Rogan pulled back and looked at her. "The Galahad half of me wants to strangle you, but the rogue wants to make love to you."

"I don't know much about Galahads," she whispered, "but I think I like this rogue. Why is he holding back?"

"Because you aren't ready for this. Because you just escaped from your father, and you've mixed me up with some fantasy sea captain—"

"And aren't you?"

"I don't know what I am, Carolina Evans, and I intend to go very slowly until we both know."

"Will you kiss me, Rogan?"

"Dammit, I shouldn't. I won't." But she looked up at him with such trust, such desire, he couldn't resist her. . . .

WHAT ARE *LOVESWEPT* ROMANCES?

They are stories of true romance and touching emotion. We believe those two very important ingredients are constants in our highly sensual and very believable stories in the *LOVESWEPT* line. Our goal is to give you, the reader, stories of consistently high quality that may sometimes make you laugh, sometimes make you cry, but are always fresh and creative and contain many delightful surprises within their pages.

Most romance fans read an enormous number of books. Those they truly love, they keep. Others may be traded with friends and soon forgotten. We hope that each *LOVESWEPT* romance will be a treasure—a "keeper." We will always try to publish

LOVE STORIES YOU'LL NEVER FORGET
BY AUTHORS YOU'LL ALWAYS REMEMBER

The Editors

Loveswept® 571

Sandra Chastain
Scarlet Butterfly

BANTAM BOOKS
NEW YORK · TORONTO · LONDON · SYDNEY · AUCKLAND

SCARLET BUTTERFLY

A Bantam Book / October 1992

*LOVESWEPT® and the wave design are registered
trademarks of Bantam Books, a division of
Bantam Doubleday Dell Publishing Group, Inc.
Registered in U.S. Patent
and Trademark Office and elsewhere.*

*If you would be interested in receiving protective vinyl
covers for your Loveswept books, please write to this address
for information:*

Loveswept
Bantam Books
P.O. Box 985
Hicksville, NY 11802

ISBN 0-553-44269-4

Published simultaneously in the United States and Canada

*Bantam Books are published by Bantam Books, a division of
Bantam Doubleday Dell Publishing Group, Inc. Its trademark,
consisting of the words "Bantam Books" and the portrayal of
a rooster, is Registered in U.S. Patent and Trademark Office
and in other countries. Marca Registrada. Bantam Books, 666
Fifth Avenue, New York, New York 10103.*

PRINTED IN THE UNITED STATES OF AMERICA

OPM   0 9 8 7 6 5 4 3 2 1

One

Sean Rogan had become a man of few words, damned few words.

Particularly where his family was concerned. In fact, he hadn't spoken a word of any kind to another Rogan in more than two years—not since he'd dissolved the family corporation, divided up its assets, and accepted the decaying family home on the St. Marys River as his part of the Rogan real estate. He couldn't speak to them; the pain and disappointment had been too great.

Then an article about his resurrection of the *Scarlet Butterfly* had appeared in the *Savannah Journal*, the daily newspaper of which his brother David was editor, and he had been forced to face his family again.

Sean had successfully avoided the press and the bickering of the various factions within the family for two peaceful years, until David had broken his agreement to protect Sean's privacy by printing the story about the schooner he'd raised and restored. Now Sean found himself in the spotlight again, in the center of a controversy over ownership of the vessel. He'd be forced to do the thing he wanted most to avoid—defend himself in a court of law.

Sean Rogan had had enough of conflict and the threat of legal battles to last a lifetime.

It didn't matter that the story of the 1850's schooner would sooner or later have been published by some other newspaper. It didn't matter that his editor brother had spent a good part of the afternoon trying to explain that he'd decided if his paper covered the story, he could protect Sean, and maybe Beth, from more publicity. Sean wished he believed him, but trust was a thing of the past. David had wanted to be the first to break the story, and he'd done it, at Sean's expense.

His sister was dead because of that kind of thinking, because they'd all been too self-centered to see what they were doing to the youngest Rogan. The family might not have been aware of what their bickering was doing to Beth, but Sean should have been. His father had left the family in his care.

Now it was about to happen again. But the *Scarlet Butterfly* was his and nobody would take it away from him, no matter what the state antiquities law said. Sean had turned his back on his former life, sworn never to go to court again, for any reason. But now he'd have to.

Sean glanced into the mirror of his truck and groaned. Though there was a recent scar on the side of his face that made him look more like a pirate than an executive, he'd been forced to take on the mannerisms of the world he'd left behind. The clothes he wore were expensive, imported, uncomfortable, and hot.

September on the Georgia coast was hot as hell and, as far as Sean was concerned, almost as populated with the devil's chosen advocates, starting with Ryan, the younger brother who most shared the responsibility of their sister's death, and David, the older brother who'd drawn Sean back into the public eye. David's claim that he'd managed to fend off all the outside inquiries about the reclusive Sean Rogan, except those of one woman who claimed to be a descendent of a woman who'd vanished in 1850 on a schooner called the *Scarlet Butterfly*, fell on deaf ears.

A descendant of a woman who'd vanished on the *Scarlet Butterfly*? Sean shook his head and slid his broad shoulders from the jacket of his suit. Fruitcakes were already coming out of the woodwork.

Wiping his forehead on the sleeve of his shirt, he threaded his fingers through his shoulder-length hair, pulled it back, and secured it with a rubber band. He wondered if he might have fared better in his meeting with the state officials if he'd had a haircut.

Sean started the engine and backed the truck into the street outside the courthouse. He left Savannah behind and drove down the coast toward the sleepy little town of St. Marys, back toward the river that shared its name, toward peace and tranquillity, toward the welcoming silence that came from being utterly alone in an inaccessible place.

In spite of the oppressive heat, the farther he drove the better he felt. For several days the local weather forecasters had been tracking the third tropical storm of the season. It was moving in the direction of the Southern coast, but its destination had not yet been pinpointed. He glanced at the sky. Sunshine was already giving way to clouds riding in from the Caribbean. No matter; he'd be home long before dark.

As he turned off the intercoastal waterway, his truck was quickly swallowed up by the thick under-brush and marshy land that bordered the road. A number of people—farmers, river people, some of them very wealthy—once lived along the St. Marys. But the pull of the city and the hardships of the area had lured them away. Gradually Sean had bought up the land until he was blessedly alone. No more corporate decisions. No more threats of takeovers and buy-outs. No more courtroom drama or family disputes to settle. Just Sean Rogan, reclusive mil-lionaire, retired corporate CEO, renegade runaway. He'd run from the famous Southern family corpora-tion that had once controlled several newspapers, television stations, resorts, and a pecan business that for the last century was the basis of wealth for the Rogans, this clan that rivaled the Kennedys for airing their public sins before the world.

Alone.

At least he thought he was, until he came to the red compact rental car, abandoned in the middle of his road, blocking his way.

Carolina Evans drew in a big breath of pungent salt air and glanced dolefully around at the sharp, spiked-leaf plants and thick underbrush beside the road. When she'd left the bustling seaport city of

Savannah, Georgia to find the mysterious recluse living on the river, she hadn't known what to expect.

From the moment she'd seen the story about the millionaire who'd discovered the 1850's schooner called the *Scarlet Butterfly* in a river near the coast of Georgia, she'd become obsessed. She'd read about that ship in an old journal in her father's library, read about it and the great-great-great-great-great-great-great-grandmother who'd run away on it. Seeing the *Butterfly* for herself became the dream that had gotten Carolina through the months of the radiation therapy that had made her hair fall out and her body so tired she could hardly move.

For so long her gains had been measured in hours, then days, and finally weeks. By then the tumor was gone, but so was her strength. Just getting to the river was as far as she'd allowed herself to think. She still couldn't believe that she'd actually come.

Her father now knew that she was gone, she realized. He'd cover his hurt with anger, then come after her. She wondered how long it would take him. She was sorry she hadn't said good-bye, but she hadn't been sure she had the courage to go through with her plan. Having the most powerful attorney in the state of Texas for a father was both a blessing and a weight to carry. He'd been able to afford her medical care, but he refused to discuss the possibility that she was ready to start her life again—alone.

And she was determined to build a new life, her own life. She'd loaded up her supply of medication, flown from Houston to Atlanta, changed planes to reach Savannah, and rented a car. After an unsatisfactory conversation with the editor of the newspaper that had printed the story, she'd driven to St.

Marys and spent the night at Ridgeway Inn, the bed and breakfast that dated back to the Revolutionary War.

After several conversations about her mission, the innkeeper, Ida, had finally told her where to find the man who'd brought the ship to the surface. Confidently, Carolina had set out to see the vessel. That's all she had in mind. Then she'd call her father and let him know that she'd arrived and that she was all right.

She hadn't expected to get lost.

But the asphalt road had changed into a black dirt road that had gradually narrowed. Now trees with huge limbs, laced overhead like fingers, closed out the last of the early-evening light and dangled long tassels of gray moss over the rental car. There had been no place to turn around. The ground fell away from the road into what smelled and looked, in the fading light, like a saltwater marsh.

The car had sputtered and died, leaving her stranded in a green swamp that seemed to breathe like a live thing ready to devour her if she stepped off the road. It was getting late. She considered her situation. There had been no houses for miles. Still, overhead she could see a power line. Power lines took electricity somewhere.

Carolina had been determined, but now she was very tired, and she wondered if her doctor and her friends had been right when they'd pleaded with her not to leave her father's house. They'd warned her that she wasn't ready to be on her own yet.

"No," she whispered, shoring up her waning strength. They were wrong. She wasn't strong yet, but the doctors had fixed her body. Now she had to mend her psyche. She'd been so tired for so long without knowing why. When her problem had finally been diagnosed as a cyst at the base of her pituitary gland, they'd operated. The growth hadn't been malignant, but she had required radiation therapy, followed by months of medication adjustment and careful monitoring in the hospital, before being transferred home and to her father's care.

Angus Evans, who had always been overprotective, had become a warden, and she'd felt as if she were slowly being smothered. Finally one morning she'd decided that she had to get away. She'd promised herself that she was going to see the *Scarlet Butterfly*, and the time had come to go.

"I'd rather you didn't leave," her doctor had argued when she'd confided her plans. "But I understand. As long as you take your medication I expect you'll do fine. Just don't overexert yourself."

"Why on earth would you leave a place where you have servants and an unlimited allowance?" her best friend had asked when Carolina had confided that she was considering moving out.

She hadn't told her father. He would have said that he knew what was best for her. And he'd promise that someday, when they were sure . . .

That someday, she knew, would never come. But he'd expect her to agree with his plan anyway, because she always had—except once, when she'd been determined to go away to college. In the end, he'd been right about that too.

It had been early in her illness that Carolina had found the journal among her mother's books in the library. From the moment she'd read it and discovered that the woman writing was also named Carolina, she'd been fascinated by the ancestor who'd run away from her powerful Boston family with a sea captain. Angus Evans had shrugged off her questions, saying he didn't know where the journal had come from, nor did he care. Yes, Carolina carried the same name, but it was simply a coincidence, he'd insisted.

Carolina knew he was wrong. And when she saw the newspaper story about the newly discovered schooner called the *Scarlet Butterfly*, she'd made up her mind. Like the first Carolina, she would strike out on her own, escape to a place where she could take control of her life. She was as well now as she was going to get. All she needed was time. What she did with the rest of her life was up to her.

It might not be the same schooner as the one the first Carolina had run away on, but it could be. She'd had to find out. And so she'd come here.

Carolina resolutely crawled out of the car and started down the road. Overhead she could see a sliver of light now and then, but the trees were so thick that the sky was hidden. She was hot and unbelievably weary. Her trek quickly turned into agony when she was attacked by hordes of mosquitoes and enveloped by an absolute stillness in which not a breath of air moved.

In the hospital she would have taken a nap to recoup her strength. Now, forcing herself to put one foot in front of the other, she kept going. Gradually she became adjusted to the sounds of the birds and swamp creatures and settled down into a kind of peaceful acceptance. The biting insects seemed to lose interest, and her fear changed into a curious kind of waiting. Somewhere ahead of her was sanctuary. She felt its pull. She'd get there. She was too close to fail.

She didn't know how far she'd walked when it happened. Suddenly she became dizzy, disoriented. Carolina didn't see anyone ahead in the road. She didn't hear anyone. She might even have dreamed the strange man who suddenly appeared beside her. One minute he wasn't there, the next he was standing in the shadows with a scowl on his face. She saw his strong profile clearly as she crumpled in his arms.

"What the . . . ? Who are you, lass? How'd you get here? How the bloody hell did you find me?"

The captain, wearing an old-fashioned navy pea coat, held the frail, half-conscious young woman and continued to swear. He was speaking aloud, he thought in amazement, though his voice was rusty and the girl didn't seem to hear. What was happening made no sense. Finally he looked around and, as if resolved to play out the familiar role of protector again, stomped off down the road carrying the girl.

He didn't know what she was doing on the road, but maybe he'd been given a second chance to fulfill his vow. Promises were sacred trusts that forever bound a person. But this woman? No, it couldn't be.

A colorful string of complaints followed by a long silence and finally by the smell of pipe tobacco intruded on the peaceful afternoon.

Sean was sweating. He'd been forced to abandon his car and walk. Now his imported Italian shoes were rubbing blisters on feet that had worn nothing more close-fitting than running shoes or moccasins for longer than he could remember. And his temper was stretched to the breaking point when he finally reached the schooner.

"Who's there?" he demanded, climbing the ramp to the boat.

There was no answer.

Sean stepped on board and stopped, listening carefully. No human sound broke the silence. There was only the lap of the water against the hull and the gentle movement of the deck beneath his feet. Even the river creatures were silent. Still, there was something, some presence. He felt a curious prickling sensation, as if everything had stopped to wait, as if he were being watched.

That sensation caught and held him. Normally he would have charged across the deck and below, but now he paused. If someone was hiding, it would hardly be a smart move for him to announce his actions. He didn't even have a weapon. Though he doubted seriously that a criminal would rent a car and drive into the swamp to commit mayhem, he'd long ago accepted that he'd lost touch with the way people think.

Patiently he forced himself to reconnoiter the deck. Though it was still light, beneath the trees the shadows cast a secretive green haze that concealed and changed the shape of the ship, turning familiar structures into ghostly objects.

Even the air seemed different. There was a suggestion of fragrance that he couldn't quite identify at first. Then it came to him. Pipe tobacco. The smell confirmed his suspicion. Someone had either come and gone or was still waiting below. Quietly Sean slipped his feet out of his shoes and let his jacket and shirt fall to the deck.

A weapon. He needed something with which to defend himself. He hadn't spent the last year painstakingly floating and restoring the schooner to have some burglar invade his privacy. Lord knew his condo in the city had been broken into. His car had been stolen. Once he'd even had his pocket picked. But this was different. This was personal, and his pulse throbbed with fury at the thought that someone had violated his sanctuary.

He withdrew a hammer from the toolbox which he'd been using to work on the planking. On cat's feet he crept across the quarterdeck and down the steps, his heart catching painfully in his throat at every creak. With any luck, whoever was waiting below wouldn't be able to distinguish his presence from the normal groans of the old ship.

Then a shrill screech cut through the air, almost causing Sean to drop his hammer. Bully. The contrary parrot who shared the ship with Sean suddenly came to life. "Ahoy there, matey. Furl t'gallant!"

The thought crossed Sean's mind that if there was an outside presence on board, Bully, who'd been left in the galley, should have been protesting like crazy. But he hadn't until now. Was the bird responding to Sean's presence, or had the intruder made a move?

Just as quickly as he'd come to life, the bird hushed. Even spookier, Sean thought. Bully had a mind of his own. He was a foul-mouthed renegade who insisted on doing his thing, much like Sean. There was no love between the two, merely the tolerance of two adversaries who recognized in each other a kindred spirit.

Sean moved down the steps, bypassing the galley, reasoning that Bully wouldn't have hushed if the intruder were there. The door to the captain's quarters was closed. Sean was certain he'd left it open. He'd found his thief. But how to proceed? By opening the door he would expose himself to whoever waited beyond. Yet there was no other way.

Holding his breath, Sean pressed his ear against the door. Nothing. The thickness of the wood protected the intruder, and, he decided, himself as well. Surprise was his best offense. He'd simply rush the man and take his chances. Taking a deep breath, he raised the hammer and opened the door.

To silence.

To a cabin that smelled, not of tobacco as he'd expected, but of . . . wildflowers? Sean allowed his eyes to grow accustomed to the shadows and waited, ready to meet the intruder.

There was a creak in the floor, as if someone had shifted his weight. Sean immediately turned toward the sound. But, other than a curious shadow, there was nothing. The cabin was empty. He took a step deeper inside the room. There was no place for a person to hide, except perhaps beneath the bed.

The floor creaked again.

Then the sheet moved, and he heard a sound of shallow breathing that seemed to come from the bed. Sean closed his eyes and opened them. Yes, there was a shape beneath the covers. What kind of burglar took time to take a nap? he wondered.

"Shades of *Goldilocks and the Three Bears!*" he whispered, and moved closer. With the hammer still raised, he clasped the sheet and slowly lowered it.

It was a woman. No, a pale, fairylike creature,

some mythical spirit who had wandered onto his ship and was sleeping in his bed.

Her skin resembled fine porcelain, faintly tinted, but clearly too fragile to be touched. Short, light-colored hair like wisps of silk lay across his pillow. Her eyes were closed in sleep, eyes with long, delicate, golden lashes that made the fantasy complete.

One slender arm was extended toward him, her hand placed in such a way that she almost seemed to be pleading. She was wearing something silk, a slip perhaps, cream-colored and so sheer that he could see the outline of her small breasts faintly rising and falling with each breath.

Sean felt a rush of disorientation, déjà vu almost. He blinked, then lowered his arms as he realized how he would look if the woman opened her eyes.

Not Goldilocks, he decided, but Sleeping Beauty, waiting to be awakened with a kiss. But what the hell was she doing in his bed? And since when did mythical fairy princesses drive red rental cars?

Maybe he was hallucinating. Maybe he'd suffered heat stroke on his way back to the river. Maybe this was all a bad dream and he'd wake up and find that nobody had written about his restoring the schooner. All this was just another mystery.

Sean blamed the unexplained sounds and smells on age, on natural shrinkage and expansion, even on the ship's name. If the captain had only called her something reasonable—"not," he whispered, "the *Scarlet Butterfly*."

The *Scarlet Butterfly*. Carolina smiled in her sleep. She was dreaming about the fierce-looking man who'd brought her there and put her to bed. She'd known even as he growled at her that he was concealing his kindness with his curses.

Now, without opening her eyes, she knew that he was back. She had to thank him, apologize for fainting in his arms. With great determination she forced open her eyes and smiled.

"Thank you, Captain. Even if you are a dream, you're just what I expected you to be."

"Well, I didn't expect you." Sean's voice thundered across the small confines of the cabin. "Who are you, and what the hell are you doing here?"

"I'm Carolina," she whispered softly, "I was looking for the *Butterfly*, and you brought me here."

Her eyelids fluttered closed, and he could tell from the sound of her breathing that she was sleeping again. He'd brought her? The woman was some kind of nut. A regular fruitcake. Then he remembered his brother's words.

A woman who claimed that one of her ancestors had disappeared on the *Scarlet Butterfly*.

Well, he'd just take care of that, and quickly. No woman was going to intrude on his life, not when he already had the courts and the historians to fend off. He'd just take her back to town and—

How? He'd had to leave his truck a good mile back. He'd have to carry her. To make matters worse, a predicted advancing storm now seemed to manifest its presence with a rumble of thunder in the distance. As if on cue, the wind picked up and the ship began to dip and sway as the air currents announced the impending storm.

Perspiration began to roll down Sean's face as the humidity grew more intense. He'd turned the ship's forecastle into his living quarters, complete with a window fan that wasn't operating and would only have circulated hot air if it were on. At least a good rain shower would cool the air. He glanced over at his unwelcome guest again and felt his pulse quicken. The storm might help bring down the temperature, but something about this woman was raising his.

She wasn't the kind of statuesque beauty he was normally attracted to. Yet even as he warred with himself over what to do, a flicker of heat blazed to life somewhere above his knees and spread upward, forcing his attention to a part of his body that welcomed the visitor in spite of his strong misgivings.

Physical manifestations were new to Sean. Always before, when frustrating moods of despair swept over him, he'd wrestle the demons of discord by pacing the deck. He'd think of Beth, his beautiful sister who'd died because he'd been too busy to see what was happening. He'd focused his anger on the family, most directly on his brother Ryan, who'd been closest to Beth and should have known. But those kinds of bad moments had occurred less and less often in the last year.

Until now.

The girl in his cabin wasn't Beth, though she was small like his sister had been. And this night the air smelled of flowers. There was no hint of the tobacco scent that periodically permeated the air around the ship. He'd decided that long ago the *Butterfly* must have carried tobacco in its hull and that its fragrance had permeated the timbers. There was no other logical explanation, except for intruders.

Sean turned and climbed the companionway steps to the deck, just as the clouds opened and the rain began to fall. It was a cooling rain, but a brisk wind slapped the drops against his bare chest like stinging sand. Sean peeled off his trousers and underwear and stood completely nude, his head thrown back, letting the water wash over him until he was calm again.

All right. So there was a woman in his bed. She wasn't after him or his body, or she wouldn't have gone back to sleep. Because she was thin and pale, he wondered if she'd been ill or in prison. Perhaps she was still sick. He couldn't take her back in a storm. And he couldn't stay on deck in the rain.

Striding into the galley, he pulled on a shirt he'd left hanging on the back of a chair. He'd have to go below for pants. Suppose he woke her? He hesitated, finally deciding that this was his ship; the shirt was enough. He uncovered Bully, who cocked his head and made a crude comment about what he would like Sean to do with himself.

"Watch it, old boy. I didn't think I left you covered. But you do remember the story about the blackbirds, don't you? I don't know much about making bird pies, but I could turn you into parrot stew."

Bully seemed unusually subdued. As if he knew about the woman, he remained quiet.

Sean made a pot of coffee, grilled a cheese sandwich, and listened to the radio as the storm intensified. Hurricane Circe—appropriate name, he thought—wouldn't hit land, but the weather system would kick up enough rain to make the river rise.

He'd already checked the moorings, extending the linkage to allow for the rising water. Though he was anchored to a dock on a small saltwater lake, the lake was fed by the St. Marys River, which joined the

Atlantic a few miles south. Because the ocean was so close, the lake and the river were subject to the ocean's tides. Often a storm swept in from the sea and played havoc with the river and its inhabitants, as it did now with the *Butterfly*.

Damn! After a long, hot, quiet summer, the season was about to change. And the thing that Sean Rogan hated most in life was change.

As predicted, the storm had settled offshore. They'd be lucky this time, catching only the fringe rain that accompanied it. Sean checked the masts again and secured the inner workings of the schooner. He was tired and wet, and even a little cold.

Cold. The woman. She was covered only by a sheet.

He covered the distance to his quarters in a second, then slowed to a tiptoe as he reached the bed. In the darkness he could hear her, but he couldn't see without a light and he was reluctant to wake her. Cautiously, he reached out and touched her shoulder.

Icy cold.

Damn, he didn't want her around, but he didn't want her to freeze to death either. He searched for a blanket, found one, and covered her. She didn't move, didn't respond to his touch or the noise he was making. Maybe she was dead.

Sean groaned. If he wasn't already in the spotlight, he would be if some woman had sneaked on board and died. The press would rehash all the painful events of the Rogans' lives, including the death of his sister. No, this intruder couldn't be dead. He heard her breathing. But she wasn't warming up, either.

When a second blanket made no change, he took a chance and shook her.

"Hey, Sleeping Beauty, are you okay?"

Her only response was a moan and a single word that she whispered over and over.

He leaned down, touching her lips with his ear before he could understand.

"Cold—cold."

He'd never wanted a phone, never needed one. Until now. He couldn't get to his truck without exposing her to the elements and more shock.

As a blast of cold air swept across the cabin, physically shoving him to his knees on the bed, the answer came to him. Almost without a thought he shed his shirt, swept back the covers, and slid beneath them, pulling the woman into his arms. Heat could be transferred body to body, even to someone suffering from exhaustion and chills.

Sean began to massage the woman—gently, once he felt the fragility of her body. The silk garment was all she was wearing; no panties, no bra—though a cursory examination of her body suggested that she had little use for a bra.

Her head found a place beneath his chin and nestled there, her soft hair a faint tickle on his chest. He shifted her, pulling her even farther over his body. Her right arm fell limply beside her, the other curled around his neck.

Sean took a deep, ragged breath. He was suddenly doing his part to raise the temperature in the room. More than that, his body was proffering its own rhythmic massage, pulsating against the inner part of the woman's thigh, in spite of his attempts to still his response.

Although she showed no awareness of what was happening, gradually a slow warmth crept over her skin. She was coming back to life, and Sean wondered briefly what she'd do if he allowed himself free reign to hasten the process.

Outside, the storm continued, the wind whipping from one direction for a while, then changing to the other. The *Butterfly* rode the turbulence well, almost as if there were a hand on the wheel helping her.

The girl shifted. Sean caught her and pulled her higher, then let her slide back to her former position. The movement caught her slip and held it around her waist, allowing the soft curls of her pubic hair to tangle with his own. Her nipples pressed into his chest. Her breath came in little puffs now, and he felt it whisper against his neck.

Almost without his being aware of it, he moved his arm farther over her, across her back, curling his fingertips over one small breast. Beneath the silk garment he felt her nipple pucker, and the corresponding jerk of response in that portion of his anatomy caught between them.

Sean groaned and tried to adjust their positions. But the movement only brought him closer to the part of her that he wanted most desperately to explore.

He felt such a tightening, such primitive lust, such overwhelming desire that it was all he could do to stop himself from rolling the woman on her back and plunging inside her. The thought of making love to her took over his mind and, like a physical presence, pressed against his temples, bringing pain.

Pain that jerked him back to reality.

Pain that sliced through him and for one moment

brought a sense of great loss. He didn't know whether the tears on his cheeks were his or had fallen from the face pressed against him. But he felt the wetness, and as if he were in some distant place, he struggled back.

"It's all right," he whispered, caressing her breast and her lower back and leg. "I won't hurt you. I didn't take care of Beth, but I'll take care of you." He repeated the reassurances over and over again, until at last he, too, was calm. And without knowing that he was doing so, Sean closed his eyes and slept.

The parrot, mysteriously covered once more, remained uncharacteristically quiet.

The storm raged through the night. Limbs broke off and fell to the ground. Logs and pieces of timber thrashed by the water slammed against each other and swirled back the way they'd come. The river rose and spilled over its banks, flooding the road and washing the lightweight red car into the rising swamp.

The ship rode the changing currents, cushioning the two passengers like a cocoon. Finally the wind calmed, leaving only a steady rain that pelted the deck in a symphony of gentle sound.

The scents of pipe tobacco and wildflowers permeated the cabin. The woman slept, sensing that she was safe, protected, cherished. The *Scarlet Butterfly* fluttered on the tips of the waves, and eventually, just before dawn, became still.

Two

Carolina dreamed they were in a hammock, she and her imaginary lover. Their bed moved back and forth, folding them together so that she was lying on top of him. She sighed in contentment and rubbed her face on his chest, relishing the caress of springy hair on her cheek.

"Nice," she whispered, feeling his knee slide between her legs. She'd dreamed of him before, her captain, but never so vividly, nor with such pleasure.

She felt warm and safe, treasured by his touch as his fingertips left the breast they'd been holding and moved lower. A warm breeze nuzzled her hair—no, not a breeze, but his breath, which, like her own, had quickened.

"See," she wanted to say to her disbelieving friends, to the father who'd protected her as long as he could by selecting her friends, subduing her will, and ignoring her when she'd voiced the need to stand on her own two feet. He meant well. He loved her. After her mother died he'd showered all his love on Carolina. But now that her illness had been conquered, that love was killing her.

See, I knew I'd find something—*it, him.*

With a wiggle, she adjusted her body so that his hand could slide lower, to the coil of heat that was spinning outward. More, she decided, wanting him to cover her with the hardness of his body. Wanting . . .

As if he'd heard her speak, he slid her from his body to her back and turned to follow her. His lips planted little moist kisses down the side of her face. His hands touched and examined and sought out every spot that gave her pleasure.

Carolina had always wanted to believe that she could feel such sensations. She'd always hoped that her father was wrong when he'd tell her she was too delicate to lead the life of a normal woman. But for a very long time, she'd believed him.

Until she'd found out that he'd lied about her imaginary childhood illnesses. There'd been nothing out of the ordinary wrong with her then. He'd been overprotective out of fear, because he hadn't wanted to lose her.

Carolina moaned and timidly reached out to touch the body of the lover who'd come to her in a dream. His bare skin felt warm and wonderfully real. Braver now, she allowed her fingers to move up his neck, across a face prickly with the stubble of a beard, and upward to full lips that parted and captured a fingertip.

She gasped. He pulled gently, sucking, setting off waves of pleasure that ran down her arm and collided with the sensation moving upward from the place his fingers had found.

Her body seemed to vibrate. She couldn't hold herself still as she felt the pressure of his fingertips, fanning over her stomach and below, cautiously, as if she were fragile, in danger of being bruised.

"More," she whispered. She wanted more. Pulling her finger free, she skimmed her hand down, ruffling the chest hair, the coarser thatch below, until she reached—

Carolina came suddenly awake. Her gaze met a pair of startled eyes directly over her, brown eyes, eyes so brown that even the watery light spilling from behind her couldn't penetrate their darkness.

He wasn't a dream lover. He was real.

"What the hell?" he said, pulling away and dragging the coverlet to the floor as he stood.

Carolina let out a little scream and skittered back against the cabin wall. "What are you doing? Where are your clothes?"

Sean followed the woman's gaze with horror. What had he been doing? The last thing he remembered was trying to warm her. Warm her? Maybe, but he was the one who was hot and aroused—and horrified.

"My clothes? Lady, these are my sleeping quarters, and I sleep buck naked every night. I believe I'd be correct in saying that it's you who is out of place. How'd you get here, in my bed?"

Carolina didn't know how to answer. There was much that she didn't know, including why the man who'd rescued her, taken her into his bed, and cared for her so tenderly was talking to her as if he were a monk and she'd just stormed the monastery walls.

"It was you," she whispered, grabbing for the sheet and trying to force out words that seemed to hang in her throat. "You rescued me and brought me here."

"Me? Rescue you?" He stiffened, muttering a curse. "If trying to bring you back from the dead is rescuing you, I apologize."

"You should." Relief turned her muscles weak and evaporated her thought process.

Sean stared at her. Lord, she was beautiful. All he wanted to do was reclaim his place in the wonderful dream from which he'd been jerked. His intense disappointment was out of character and out of control.

"I'm thinking it would have served you right if I'd dumped you overboard in the storm and let the river wash you out to sea."

She gasped, and he knew he'd been too harsh. He wasn't angry with her—it was his actions that had unsettled him.

"Now just a minute, Mr. . . . what is your name?"

"Rogan, just Rogan, as if you didn't know," he snapped, trying to gather his senses.

He'd been wrong when he'd called her Sleeping Beauty. Sleeping Beauty was much too passive. His first impression, the adventurous Goldilocks, was more like it. Even now, after waking in bed with a strange man, her face flushed with passion, she wasn't backing down.

"I didn't," she said, straightening her shoulders defiantly. "But if you're Sean Rogan, you're the man I've come to see."

Given the absurdity of the situation, her choice of words elicited a genuine laugh. He was beginning to enjoy her brave demeanor. "So you've come to see me? Then look, because I'm not in a position to hide much."

He wasn't. She had to hand it to him: He didn't even try. He was magnificently male. The erection gradually subsided, though his size was still—arresting. Any other man might have been embarrassed at the diminishing physical expression of his manhood, but not Rogan. He simply rocked back and forth on the balls of his feet and waited.

"I'd like to get up now, Rogan," Carolina began. "I find it exceedingly difficult to carry on a reasonable discussion under the circumstances."

"Yes, it's the circumstances that I'd like to talk about—you in my bed, in my arms—"

"Yes, well, it wasn't my doing," she snapped. "What did you do with my clothes?"

"I did nothing with your clothes. Your slip seems to be in place, if you lower it from around your neck. I don't know where you came from, but dressed like that, you must have really had an interesting going-away party."

Carolina felt her composure give way. Fencing words with this dark-haired, angry man was well and good, but she was woefully inexperienced in foreplay, wordplay, or male-female play in general.

But what had just happened between them had been a two-way street. She'd been giving as much as he, and the sudden separation was causing a physical reaction not unlike the one that occurred when her medication needed repeating.

His surprise was as evident as her own, though she couldn't understand why he claimed not to know what had happened to her clothes, or how she'd gotten there. She might not have known the name,

but those strong arms had brought her on board
and—

On board, he'd said. The schooner. "I'm on the
Scarlet Butterfly?"

He nodded. "Of course. Isn't that what you intended?"

"Oh, yes. Yes! Yes! I made it!"

His brother had been right. This had to be the
woman—the fruitcake who'd asked all the questions. Sean shook his head and turned to rummage
in a drawer for a pair of clean shorts. He stepped into
them and pulled them up his muscular legs with
little regard for his audience.

"You made it," he agreed. "Too bad your car didn't.
It would have saved me a long, hot walk. I'll be in the
galley. There's a bathroom through that door, or
what passes for one on a ship. I'll give you five
minutes to get out of my bed and join me. I want
some explanations."

Carolina watched him leave the room adjusting
the waist of his shorts. She felt the tension, as well
as the temperature, drop as he left. At least he'd
decided to admit that he'd brought her. So he had
been sleeping when he'd . . . Well, she'd been sleeping too. She let out a long, uneven breath and felt her
body complain over the loss of comfort. No, if she
were honest, it wasn't comfort that it wanted—it was
something more. Suddenly the idea of dressing appealed to her, as did as the smell of coffee that came
wafting down the steps a short time later.

Coffee, and was that pipe tobacco? Too bad. Smoking was a bad habit for such a fine specimen of a
man. Carolina sighed. Who was she to caution him
about health? She'd never done anything to make

herself ill, but she had been anyway. Still, except for the loss of some weight and a lot of hair, which was only now beginning to grow back, she'd survived.

A glance around the cabin didn't reveal her clothes. The only garment available was Rogan's shirt, crumpled in a wrinkled mass on the floor. She slid her arms into the sleeves and pulled the front together. The tail of the shirt fell to her knees, and there was enough room inside the buttoned garment for two women her size. In the tiny bathroom she used Rogan's comb to straighten her hair, thought about borrowing his toothbrush, and settled for a bit of paste on her finger instead.

She was down on her knees in the cabin looking under the bed for her shoes when she realized that he'd returned. Even then she had the crazy thought that she might be dreaming, for he suddenly seemed different. Standing in the shadows of the companionway, just out of full view, he held a pipe in his hand as he watched her.

"I guess you don't know where my shoes are, either?"

"In the chest. But you won't need them. My ship is quite comfortable. Are you all right?"

"If you mean the state of my health, yes. If you're referring to your assault on my body, I'm not sure. Perhaps we ought to talk about that."

She opened the chest and found her clothes. Why hadn't he said where he'd put them in the beginning? With a sigh of relief, Carolina turned a questioning face back to the companionway.

He was gone.

But he was right about the shoes; the floor was polished and smooth. And her clothes looked hot and out of place. If she removed her slip, Rogan's shirt would cover her like a short dress, except for the deep vee above the top button. Formality suddenly seemed a bit foolish as she remembered what they'd shared. She took off the slip and buttoned the shirt.

Carolina tucked the slip under the pillow and pulled up the covers before starting for the galley and the smell of coffee. A steady patter of rain fell on the deck overhead. She had to dash across an open area to the on-deck portion of the living quarters that made up the galley.

"Awwwk? Hot damn, she's a beauty!"

Carolina came to an abrupt stop.

"Looky, looky, looky, here's nooky!"

"Shut up, you bald, beaked buzzard," Rogan snapped, "or I'll pluck you and eat you for dinner!"

"Awwwk! Try it, scabby!"

Carolina looked from the man drinking coffee at the table to the cage swinging from the ceiling.

"A parrot?"

"He claims to be a nightingale. But then, he lies a lot."

"Oh, ho ho, and a bottle of beer."

Of course there'd be a parrot. "Beer?" she asked with a smile. "I thought it was a bottle of rum. May I have a cup?"

"Not a drop of rum on board, Goldilocks. What happened to your hair?"

"I meant coffee," she corrected, and glanced out the open door at the water. "I shaved my head. It's just growing back."

"Why, are you some kind of rebel?"

She smiled. A rebel? Her? Not until now. "In a

way, I suppose," she said, with a certain amount of pride. "It looks like the river is moving awfully fast."

"It isn't the river, it's a lake. Well, actually, I suppose it's both now. Technically, I guess you'd call this a flood. We caught the edge of a hurricane."

"Will we be all right?"

"Sure. The dock is underwater, and I don't even want to think about your rental car, but the *Butterfly* can handle almost anything."

Sean poured a cup of coffee and handed it to Carolina, who was wearing his shirt as if it belonged to her. Their hands touched and he felt her jerk back, then cry out as the coffee sloshed over the rim and across her fingers.

Quickly, he took the cup and set it on the table. He wet a cloth, sat, and pulled her between his thighs while he cleaned the coffee from her hand. He fought the urge to kiss away the pain and tried not to notice the electricity that arced between them.

"It's okay," she whispered.

But it wasn't. And he didn't know why. He was holding her captive with his body. She looked frightened, yet she didn't pull away. There were circles under her eyes, but the dark smudges didn't detract from the fine bone structure of her lovely face. She was beautiful. Her delicate face was oval, with a small aristocratic nose that turned up at the end in a dare.

"I'm really all right," she said quietly, stepping away.

She reclaimed her cup and filled it again. Eyes too large and too bright for his comfort looked at him over the edge of the cup as she sipped the hot liquid. They were a cool, silvery green, almost gray, like the river in shadows. He wondered if she could sense the undercurrents bouncing about the galley, and decided that she could. Most women would fill the silence with words, he thought; most women wouldn't be able to exist in a void washed with such vivid sensations.

Sean cleared his throat.

"That was your car back on the road?"

"Yes, I think I ran out of gas. I'll call a service station, if you'll let me use your phone."

"No phone. I doubt anybody would come anyway. The current is still rising. Looks like neither of us is going anywhere."

"I'm sorry. It's just that I need my clothes."

"I'm afraid you're out of luck until the storm lets up. But"—he gave her a long, heated look—"you're welcome to wear anything I have—or nothing at all, if you choose."

"Thanks. I did find the suit I was wearing when I came, but it seemed awfully heavy. Did you get wet earlier?"

"Wet? A little. Why?"

"Well, just now, in the stairway, I thought you'd changed clothes. Were you wearing something blue?"

"In the companionway? Look, Goldilocks, you're still weak or something. I've been right here, except for my attempt to find the dock." His voice sharpened again, revealing his tension.

"Mr. Rogan, I'm very sorry. I seem to keep making you angry, and I'm not sure why. Maybe we got off to a bad start. Let me introduce myself. My name is Carolina Evans."

Bad start? He had to bite back a colorful swear. She had inserted herself in his solitary, orderly life as if she'd been expected, and now was embroidering on her plans by pretending that they shared some secret. Still, there was something utterly compelling about her, something that appealed to the protective side of his nature. He felt responsible for her, and at the same time guilty over the desire she fostered without even knowing she was doing so.

"So, Carrie," he said awkwardly, in an attempt to regain control of a situation that seemed to deteriorate into pure lust every time they touched, "can you cook?"

CARRIE?

The table rocked violently for a moment. Carolina and Sean caught the edge and steadied it.

"Did we hit something?" she asked.

There was a puzzled expression on Rogan's face as he stood, glanced out the window, and turned back. "Must have been a swell, or maybe a log. Don't worry, the *Butterfly* is safe."

Their gazes met and caught for a long moment. "I knew it would be, Mr. Rogan. That's what drew me here. But I didn't expect you, or intend to—I mean I should thank you for caring for me."

"Forget the 'mister.' I think we're past that. I apologize for what happened. I don't usually sleep with a woman who doesn't even know I'm there, but you'd turned into an icicle, and I didn't know any other way to warm you. Then I fell asleep too."

She took another sip of coffee and felt its heat slide down her throat. "Funny, I wasn't cold when I woke up."

Was she kidding? If they'd been any warmer, they'd have incinerated the sheets. But the uncertainty in her eyes cut through his hormonal reaction and he forced himself to back off.

"I was pretty warm, myself. If I'd known what I was doing, I wouldn't have. I wouldn't want you to—Hell, I don't know what I mean. But if you were offended, I'm sorry!"

"I don't think I was," she admitted in a low, shy voice. "I think that I rather enjoyed it. Do you bring women here often?"

Sean leaned forward, caught the edges of the shirt that dangled loosely on her, and drew them together under her chin so that the opening covered the pulse in her neck. "You're the first woman to ever set foot on board the *Scarlet Butterfly*, Carolina, but I didn't bring you."

"But I distinctly remember. I got very dizzy. I'm not accustomed yet to doing much walking, and it was so hot. Just as I collapsed, you caught me, and I must have fainted. I vaguely remember you undressing me and putting me in your bunk, then nothing else until you—I—this morning . . . Was that—what you were doing—foreplay?"

Sean felt the air whoosh out of his lungs. Here they were standing almost thigh to thigh in his tiny galley, and she was looking up at him as if he had all the answers and she needed every one of them.

"Ahh, Carolina. This is a very strange encounter. You must have dreamed it. I think you have a vivid imagination. You're—you're little more than a child, and you're much too trusting."

"I'm twenty-five and I know I'm too trusting. I'm a sucker for Girl Scout cookies and band candy. I buy chances on new cars and every time Ed McMahon sends me a letter, I subscribe to another magazine. I mean I'd feel terrible if I won the grand prize and hadn't ordered anything. Wouldn't you?"

Sean didn't even know how to answer. If she'd feel bad about winning a contest when she hadn't bought a magazine, how would she feel about building up to making love and then stopping short of the final act? He swallowed hard as he realized that she was still waiting for an answer.

"That was foreplay. Haven't you made love before?"

"No, at least not anything like that. What you did was very . . . stimulating. My only experience was more like a poor simulation."

"Simulating foreplay?" *Only experience*? That idea blew his mind. What was she saying? That she'd only had one lover and he'd been inept? That was something Sean had never been accused of. And if the reaction he'd gotten was any measure of it, Carolina was a lady more than capable of responding.

She was studying him earnestly. "I think I'd like to discuss this further, Captain. I'll need to think about it. Would you like some breakfast?"

Sean simply stared at her. He wasn't certain that he'd answered until she turned to the refrigerator.

For Carolina, the offer to cook breakfast for Rogan was a deliberate attempt to direct his attention to another subject while she got her emotions under control. It didn't work.

All conversation stopped. Sean was still trying to interpret the concept of simulated foreplay.

Watching her move from the tiny gas cookstove to the table and back was like watching a child discovering the pieces of a dollhouse and arranging them in their proper places. She picked up the frying pan and ran her fingers across the bottom as if she'd never seen one, pleasure bringing a smile to her face. The small refrigerator beneath the counter brought another smile, as did the eggs she examined as if she'd never cracked one before.

"I'll make the toast," he said, finding something on which to focus his attention. He ought to be asking for answers. He ought to be building a raft so that he could take her back to town. But he couldn't forget the pallor of her skin, the fragility of her body, the heat that had flared between them. She wasn't well, he rationalized, and he couldn't subject her to the stress of getting back to civilization.

"Oh, is there a real toaster?"

"No, I just butter it and brown it in a skillet."

That was a mistake. One person could stand between the table and the stove, but two people filled every cubic inch of space, provided they were joined at the hip and willing to move in tandem.

Awkwardly, Carolina cut chunks of cheese in the pan.

"Are you going to put some butter in there first?" Sean asked.

"Oh, of course." She added a slab of butter and cracked the first egg directly into the pan, then the second, realizing her mistake when several pieces of shell fell on top of the yolk. It looked so easy when she watched Cook do it. But capturing and retrieving the broken shell was hard.

"Aren't you going to season them?" Sean asked.

"I'm not allowed to—" She stopped short, took the salt and pepper from the cabinet, and nodded. "Of course I'm going to season them." She shook the paper salt carton generously, studied the pan, and added more.

After vigorously stirring the mixture until she'd turned it into mutilated yellow slivers, Carolina divided the eggs on the plates, where Sean's toast had already been placed. He refilled their cups and took his seat on the only bench, indicating with one hand that she could share the space.

There was a moment of discomfort as she arranged his shirt so that she could sit without exposing more of her legs than necessary.

"I hope you don't mind my wearing your shirt."

"Not at all," he said, and took a large bite of eggs and cheese. "Feel free to wear as little as you like. That's what I do." He didn't know whether it was the overdose of salt, the crunch of eggshells, or his hormonal reaction to the thought of what was beneath that shirt that caused the food to lodge in his throat, but he swallowed wrong and began to cough.

"What's the matter? Are you choking? I'll help you!"

Carolina moved quickly behind Sean and caught his massive chest in her arms. Taking a deep breath, she gave a sudden tight squeeze that closed off the small amount of passageway still allowing him to swallow.

The woman was trying to smother him, attempting and failing. She had about as much staying power as a ladybug. He began to laugh.

In the melee that followed the bench tipped, throwing Sean backward and catching Carolina beneath him on the floor.

"Man the torpedoes, full speed ahead!" Bully squawked, flapping his wings wildly.

By the time the cabin quit lurching, Sean realized that Carolina wasn't moving. She wasn't speaking either. He whirled over, catching his elbows on the floor on either side of her.

"Are you hurt, darling?"

"'Darling'?" Carolina's eyes were closed. Her voice was dreamy and the top button of his shirt was completely gone, revealing the absence of the slip and something more.

She was acutely aware of his thighs cradling her body. "I like that," she said in a breathless whisper. "It sounds different coming from you."

"What?" He was practically whispering too. What was there about this woman that turned him into some kind of parrot? She must have hit her head. She wasn't even pushing him away. And he had no inclination to move.

"'Darling.' That's nice. Does this always happen, Captain?"

"If you mean do I always end up on top of a woman, no, I can't say that I do." The change in his body hadn't been gradual. It had been a primitive surge of intensity, and it had caught him by surprise.

"It's very—powerful, the feelings you create with your touch. You called me 'darling.' Do you—does that go along with . . . I mean, does your body always react so strongly? I think you must be a highly sexed man."

Highly sexed? He groaned. Damn! he said to himself. He was hard again, and that hardness was desperately seeking the softness of the area that had been withdrawn from him earlier.

"Damn!" Sean pushed himself up, caught Carolina by the hands, and drew her up against him. "Are you all right?"

"I think so. Shouldn't I be?"

"Then what in hell were you doing putting that wrestler's move on me?"

"That was no wrestler's move. That was the Heimlich maneuver. Weren't you choking?"

"On those mutilated eggs? No! It was the salt. Who taught you to cook?"

"Nobody," she murmured. "I've never cooked anything in my life. I'm sorry."

They were still touching, thigh to thigh, breast to chest, his hands holding her hands.

He moved a half-step away. "Carolina Evans, I'm afraid that we're stuck here, together, on this ship, for at least another day, and I have to know, are you really all right? I mean, have you been in some kind of institution? If you've run away, I'll be glad to help you, but you have to behave yourself, quit coming on to me."

Carolina gave a light laugh. "Have I run away? Yes. If you mean from a *mental* institution, no." She smiled, her eyes widening in question. "Was I really coming on to you?"

Sean groaned. "Hell, yes! I think I'll swim to shore. Don't try to cook. Don't clean the kitchen. Don't do anything until I return."

"All right," she agreed, bemusement washing her face with wonder. "I don't know much about you, Captain Sean Rogan, but I think you ought to relax and enjoy whatever life sends you. Whatever, or *who*ever. You never know when you'll lose it all. You're much too rigid."

"'Rigid'?" She was right. And his body wasn't

complying with his cease-and-desist directive. Nor was it likely to, as long as they were standing so close. To compound matters, she came closer and slid her arms up to his face, capturing it with her hands.

"You should have a captain's hat," she whispered. "He did. And she loved it."

Feeling confused enough already, he let these remarks pass.

The last thing he'd intended to do was kiss her. In fact, he couldn't remember lowering his face until their lips touched. Her lips were soft, parting hesitantly. He liked that, liked that she trusted him to lead the way—even as he realized, as he deepened the kiss, that he was taking advantage of her trust. It made no sense. But nothing had made any sense since he'd pulled back the covers and found her in his bed.

The soft little mew she let out as she melted against him jerked him back to reality. He was supposed to be taking care of her. He'd promised. And there he was, jumping all over her like some kid caught in his first attack of hormonitis. He'd let himself get too caught up in the stress of his own needs and responsibilities once before, when he'd ignored his little sister's problems. This time he ought to know better, he chided himself.

Sean shoved past Carolina onto the deck, drawing air into his lungs. "I'm going to check on your car," he called out, and disappeared over the side into the fast-moving current.

For a long moment he felt himself being swept downstream, but then his strong thrusts began moving him toward the trees that marked where the shoreline would normally have been. Sean reached up, caught hold of a limb of a live oak, and pulled himself from the water. Scanning the tree for snakes, he began to climb. The St. Marys originated in the Okefenokee Swamp. Heavy rains overflowed the swamp, bringing trash, limbs, and an occasional unwilling swamp animal along with them until just below the schooner the river current crashed into the saltwater coming inland with the tide.

From the top of the tree, he scanned where the road should have been. Though he should have been able to sight the red car through patches of leafless tree, he couldn't see anything but water. The rain was still falling, not hard but steady. Sean turned his gaze back to the boat.

There was no sign of the woman.

He perched there, trying to sort out his thoughts. Carolina Evans. He had a name, nothing more. She'd apparently come looking for him—no, not for him, but the *Scarlet Butterfly*. Why? Why the elaborate pretense that he was what she'd expected? That anything had been expected? He didn't understand, and when he didn't understand, Sean Rogan became abrupt, sharp, and, as he'd been called, "a cold-hearted bastard," more interested in having his way than in listening to others.

But Carrie—no, not Carrie; Carrie was too personal; he'd do better to think of her as Goldilocks—Goldilocks didn't seem to think he was a bastard. In fact, she seemed quite pleased with the "captain."

But what was he doing dwelling on her, when he needed so badly to focus all his attention on the fight ahead of him. He was making a mistake, he thought ruefully to himself. And so had kissing her been a mistake, as was his willingness to accept her without a better explanation.

It had to end. It was bad enough that the schooner had developed a will of its own—creaking from footsteps that weren't there, tables shuddering for no good reason, sudden breezes that swept in and died—but now he had a fantasy woman who was slipping past the hard armor he'd forged so carefully around his emotions.

Dammit, this was his boat, his domain. He might not be able to do anything about her until the storm passed, but he could set up some rules.

The first thing he needed was information.

Who was Carolina Evans, and why was she there?

Three

"Ahoy, Captain, swab the deck! Awwwk!"

Parrots! The captain listened to the bird and swore. When he'd sailed the Butterfly, *he'd never believed in having animals on a ship. Then she'd found a feisty, half-starved kitten, and he hadn't been able to refuse her request to keep him. She'd called him Barney, and long after she'd gone, Barney was still there, Barney and the child. They'd kept an uneasy peace until one day the child grew up and left. Soon Barney, too, was gone, and he was alone.*

Until now.

After all these years, the Butterfly *had been raised by another Rogan. The cat had been replaced by a bird. And a young Carolina, proud and invincible, had come back. Almost as if he'd been given another chance.*

Oblivious to the rain, he leaned against the mast and watched the young woman as she tasted the eggs and grimaced. It was obvious that she was as unfamiliar with cooking as he was with the changing banks of the river he'd once known as well as the back of his hand.

A suggestion of a smile played across Carolina's lips as she scraped the too-salty food overboard. Then she took on a look of quiet determination as she studied the cookstove and the food supplies in the storage area. Slipping a carrot from the refrigerator, she offered it to the bird.

"Hello, Bully. I bet you'd like something special for your breakfast."

Bully eyed her suspiciously for a moment, then sidled over to the edge of his perch and took the treat.

"Pretty Carrie!"

"Carolina," she corrected. "Doesn't take you long to learn. I think that the captain is a little slower. He doesn't quite know what to make of me." She leaned against the table and let out a deep sigh. "To tell the truth, neither do I. Father never believed that I would leave. But I did it."

"'Father'?" Sean Rogan stepped inside the galley and leaned against the door frame. "Then you are mortal, not some spirit come to torment me."

"Of course I'm mortal."

"If I hadn't seen your car I might question that. Why did you come here, Carolina Evans? What did you expect?"

"I don't know. I didn't think that far ahead. I came; that was enough. As soon as the water recedes, I'll leave."

He continued to eye her skeptically and to speak in a voice that was low and intentionally calm. "Where will you go? You don't look very strong. Is there someone I can call to come and get you?"

"No, I'll manage by myself."

She obviously wasn't well. Yet, like some wild thing, she was ready to fight for her independence. He admired her for her spirit and her determination. There was a softness about her too, and it reached out and touched a part of him he'd thought closed off long ago—compassion, the ability to put someone else's needs ahead of his own.

No, he wouldn't fall into the same old trap. He'd finally managed to get away from people who needed him one minute and then stabbed out at him in anger when he didn't give more of himself, people who demanded more from him than they were willing to give. He'd put up with that for too long, until one day he'd realized that there was little of himself left, that those he'd given to hadn't appreciated any of his caring, that his ability to care was gone.

"No, no, there's no one to call," she explained hesitantly. "I know this doesn't make much sense to you. I truly didn't expect anything, except to see the schooner. When I saw the story about the *Scarlet Butterfly* in the magazine, I knew it had to be the boat I'd read about."

"You read about it? Where?"

"In an old journal that was handed down in my mother's family. The schooner disappeared in eighteen sixty. There couldn't be two boats named *Scarlet Butterfly*, could there?"

"I doubt it. Boats were named for people, for spirits, even dreams, but butterflies? Our captain must have been a little . . . different."

"Oh, he was. Jacob was a rough but caring man. He must have loved Carolina very much."

"Jacob?"

"Captain Jacob Rogan, the man who sailed the *Butterfly*. A man much like you, I'd guess. Isn't it odd? I'm Carolina, but your name is different."

"Whoa! What makes you think that the man who sailed this ship was named Jacob Rogan?"

"I read it, in Carolina's daughter's journal. And even if I hadn't, I think I'd have known that you belong here. His name was Rogan; your name is Rogan. The ship once belonged to him, and you found it. I had an ancestor named Carolina, and I found you. Don't you feel the continuity? Like the circle is complete again."

As if in answer, the ship took a sudden dip, throwing Sean through the doorway onto the deck. Carolina followed, concern etched across her forehead. "Are you all right?"

"Damned if I know. You may think I belong, but I'm not sure the ship agrees."

"Oh, but if it weren't for you, the ship would still be underwater."

"Yeah, maybe that's where it wants to be."

"No, this is right. I know it."

"'Right'? Here I am, in the middle of a flood, with a woman who not only claims to know more about the ship I've spent the last two years restoring than I do, but who knows about my—my ancestors too."

"Oh, no, not really. Carolina's daughter's journal was only partially intact. I'm not even sure how she was related to me. Sometime in the last hundred years there was another flood, and most of the writing was too faded to read."

"What do you know?"

"I just know Carolina ran away with Captain Rogan on the *Scarlet Butterfly* and disappeared. Her daughter didn't write much about her childhood, just that her mother died, and she lived with the captain, who, when he went back to sea, left her with his brother in Charleston."

"Odd, my family came here from Charleston."

"Really? You know, in some weird kind of way, maybe Carolina and Rogan have come home. I like that idea, don't you?"

"Just so long as you're not planning on carrying out that second part of Carolina's history."

"You mean dying? No, that's behind me now. I intend to live, really live from now on."

"Ahoy the ship!" a voice called out, breaking Rogan's train of thought, forestalling any more questions.

"Harry!" Rogan exclaimed, and turned back to Carolina to explain. "Harry is a fisherman who lives in the swamp." Rogan climbed the stairs and moved toward the rear of the boat. "Harry, you all right?"

Carolina followed, sighting a wizened old man wearing overalls and a railroad cap.

"Yep. Just thought I'd better check on you. Pretty bad storm, weren't it, boy?" He tilted his head as he caught sight of Carolina. "Sorry, didn't know you had a lady now."

"I don't!"

Sean looked at Carolina again. "I mean she's just come about the *Butterfly*."

"Are you thinking of selling her?"

"No. I couldn't, even if I wanted to. Haven't you heard? The state's put in a claim."

"Oh?" The old man's flatboat bobbed in the water as he struggled to find a calmer spot near the shore where he could escape the unsettling swirls of water.

"They're trying to claim state ownership."

Carolina felt a chill come over her. "But they can't," she protested. "The *Scarlet Butterfly* belonged to Jacob Rogan. You must be his descendant. That makes it yours, or at least it belongs to the Rogan family."

"Yeah, well it looks as if I'm going to have to find a bill of sale to prove it."

"Too bad," Harry said. "Well, I've got to get on downstream. I want to check on Miss Lucy. You know she's got no phone on that old houseboat where she lives, and she might need something. Can I bring you anything on my way back?"

"No, but thanks," Rogan said. "We'll be fine. If it stops raining, the water will drop by morning."

Harry pushed himself away from the bank and let the current move him out. "See you in a day or so."

They watched Harry lift his steadying pole from the water, allowing his boat to be swept downstream and around the curve of land, out of sight.

"Why didn't you send me with Harry?"

Rogan looked startled.

"In a flat-bottomed boat in a fast current? Not safe. Look at you, you're getting soaked."

She was. The soft cotton shirt hugged her slim body as water dripped down her forehead. A silence fell between them, and she didn't know what to say. The raindrops no longer bounced off the deck, but fell gently on its polished surface. The wind was gone, so that the trees hung heavy with water, the limbs bending down and being dragged by the cur-

rent. Its swiftness had abated, but it was still powerful and still carried debris, slamming it against the
hull of the ship and off again in a furious chase.

Rogan set his lips sternly. He stood opposite her,
waiting for her to speak, studying her with regret
and confusion. He wished he had sent her with
Harry. It would have been a smart move. Lucy could
have taken her in until they could reclaim her car.
Or she could have gone back to Ida's in town. But he
hadn't, and he recalled with a jab in the gut that for
one second he had considered it, then had deliberately closed off the thought, further saddling himself
with this half-starved woman-child who'd boarded
the *Butterfly* and sought refuge in his bed.

Her hair was wet, plastered to her head like a
cap. Her eyes seemed more blue, a silvery blue. They
were opened wide, watching him with childlike innocence and trust. At the same time she was waiting as
if she expected to be censured and was willing to
take his rebuke. Something about that trust caught
him off guard and made him want to draw her close
and comfort her. She shivered.

"Oh, hell!"

Rogan swept her into his arms and carried her to
his quarters. "What were you thinking, standing out
there in the rain like some water sprite?"

He took a thick towel from behind the door and
began to dry her hair, to blot the moisture from her
face. To Rogan the cabin was warm, very warm, but
her skin was cool. "You're soaked, and I don't think
you're strong enough to take this kind of chill."

She nodded as he knelt down, drying her legs and
ankles.

"You've been ill, haven't you?"

"Yes."

"I thought so." He swore and began unbuttoning the shirt. "I want you back in that bed, under those covers."

"Will you come too?"

The implication of her question took his breath away and stilled his hands.

"No. You've already had a sample of what can happen. I might not have been conscious of what I was doing then, but I know better now. I'm going back on deck. You get in bed and cover up. I'll bring you some hot coffee later."

Abruptly, he left the room, climbing the steps in one long stride. Inside the cabin Carolina finished unbuttoning the shirt, draped it across the bureau, and climbed into the bunk. Clearly, he'd come to his senses, and he didn't want her. She could understand that, but the knowledge hurt. Men had never been more than a teenage fantasy—except once, when she'd learned just how far her father's money could go.

But Rogan was different. She sensed that beneath his gruff exterior he was hiding a man who could care. For a moment she allowed herself to remember the safety of his arms, the way he smelled, and the texture of his bare skin against hers. Suddenly she felt as if her skin were encased in a moving blanket of electric impulses. She clenched her teeth, pulled the covers over her, trying in vain to stay awake until he returned.

As she fell asleep, she breathed in the smell of lemon oil, the smell of rain, the smell of pipe tobacco.

• • •

When Sean brought the coffee to the cabin, she was sleeping peacefully. He studied her for a long time, then placed the cup on the table beside the bed and left the cabin. He didn't trust himself not to touch her.

And he vividly remembered the last time he had.

It was late afternoon when Sean Rogan followed the gangplank down into the water until he found the dock and walked to shore. He plunged through the palmetto palms at a rapid pace toward the remains of the old house. He didn't know why he was so angry, but he wanted to break things. Using a fallen limb, he swept the brush aside with a violence that would have served him well in a sword fight.

For the two years since he'd walked away from the Rogan empire, he'd lived on this land. At first he'd planned to restore the house. It was because of another storm and the accidental capsizing of his own small boat that he'd discovered the *Butterfly* in the lake. From the moment he'd realized what he'd found, he'd been obsessed with the thought of raising and restoring it. After months of research he'd brought in men who knew how to pump out mud and pump in air. And finally, they'd brought her to the surface.

The men had warned him that the ship wouldn't be intact, that warm water and worms would have rendered it unsalvageable. They'd been wrong. The *Butterfly* had survived for two reasons: It had been built from cypress, and some long-ago flood had encased it in protective mud. It wasn't totally without damage, but it was in much better shape than anybody had expected.

His plans to live in the house were quickly shelved

in favor of living on the boat. Storage quarters became his cabin, with a small toilet just off the bedroom. The original galley built on deck had been refurbished and served as his kitchen. There were no sails yet. The masts needed replacing, as did one section of the deck that had been destroyed by some unknown object or person.

At the house, Sean climbed the steps and entered the foyer. Mold and spiderwebs draped the remaining walls. Large holes in the roof let in the rain, and some intruder had built a fire in the middle of what was once the parlor floor.

None of the present Rogans knew much about the house, only that early ancestors had built the house on the river they had used to move their goods to market. Years later they'd planted the pecan orchards and moved to Savannah, leaving the house to fall into ruins. Sean's brothers and sisters were only too happy to let him claim the swampy acreage as his part of the family real estate. None of them wanted it. There was no money to be made in the marsh, and rice farming was a thing of the past.

Sean had felt as if he'd come home. There was something peaceful about the ruins. If he had been into spiritualism, he could have seen himself meditating in this place. Holding seances even, opening himself to the spirits of the people who'd once lived there. The original deeds for the house and land probably carried the first Rogan's name. But courthouse records with dates and names had burned long ago.

He looked around. The once-proud walls were broken, like the woman on his boat. Both needed new life. They'd both come under his care. But the house was a thing, and things could be picked up and discarded. The woman was different.

The rain stopped, leaving only the constant sound of water dripping from the tree limbs through the holes in the ceiling. The air was heavy, humid. Now tiny biting insects began to swarm, and Sean regretted not having grabbed a shirt.

A shirt.

His shirt.

The woman wearing his shirt.

Four

Carolina had hoped she was through needing so much sleep; instead, it seemed that she needed more. Once sleep had been a welcome escape from pain, from boredom, from the sameness of her illness. But this sleep was different. It came in gentle contentment. It was late afternoon when she opened her eyes and saw him standing just out of range in the doorway.

"You're always in the shadows," she said quietly. "Where you don't look quite real."

"I am not real, lass. I fear none of this is. I should not be able to converse with you."

"You're not Rogan, are you?"

"No. I'm—I'm not quite sure who I am."

"Does Rogan see you?"

"No. I think not—not yet."

"Well, you're very real to me."

"I know, and I don't like it, lass. This is all wrong— your presence here—alone—now. You're part of a

future to which I do not belong. And I will not watch you suffer again. Go back where you belong."

"Do you really want me to go?"

"Do I want? I want—no, in truth I don't wish you to go, but it's best. There can be no purpose served by any of this. It was all settled long ago. Raising the schooner was a mistake. Trust me, Carolina. This isn't right."

"But you love the *Scarlet Butterfly.*"

"Yes—that, and more."

And then he was gone, and she couldn't be sure that she hadn't dreamed him. Was the man Rogan? Something about him was different—his speech pattern, the way he kept his distance. He moved so softly. The stairs hadn't even creaked as he'd left.

Trust him, he'd asked. He didn't have to ask. For she knew that she already did. But he wanted her to go, and that was something she couldn't do—not yet.

His shirt was still damp from the rain, so when she dressed she donned her own clothes. The tailored skirt and blouse hung loose on her body. She looked at them and frowned, trying to imagine why she'd ever bought anything so tacky. The answer was that she hadn't. Her father had bought all her clothes, or he'd had someone else do it.

It hadn't always been that way. There'd been a time, once, when she'd been able to do her own choosing—her last two years of college. She'd reveled in the freedom. After two years of attending a small nearby college while she'd lived at home, she'd transferred to a university in Dallas. For two years she'd lived in the dorm like an ordinary student, taking art classes from a renowned instructor. She'd even met someone, someone who had seemed content with her.

But that was as long as the dream lasted. Just before graduation she'd come down with a headache that wouldn't go away. She'd thought it was the flu, or that maybe she was simply overworked, but it had intensified, until one day she had a seizure and awoke in the hospital. The rest was a blur of pain and disappointment.

After she'd been released from the hospital, Carolina had continued to live at home so that her doctors could monitor her condition on an outpatient basis. Void of energy and inspiration, she'd given up her art. She hadn't picked up a sketch pad in over a year. She'd been sick and so very tired for so long. Who wanted to sketch hospitals and sick people?

But suddenly, on the *Butterfly*, she could feel a spark of creative yearning come to life again. The huge live oak trees with their branches curtsying to the ground, the cypress knees, the river, the birds. She knew there'd be birds when the rain stopped, for she'd heard them calling to one another. Yes, her fingers itched for a piece of charcoal and a sketch pad.

The weather had cleared while she'd slept. But clear weather was a mixed blessing. It meant she had to leave.

Bully was squawking loudly when she entered the empty galley. A pot of something that smelled wonderful was simmering on the gas stove. The sun was shining brightly, and the air smelled fresh and clean. Carolina stepped out on the deck and looked around. The setting sun cast pink and purple shadows across the marsh as the huge orange ball slid out of sight behind the trees. As if on command, a white egret rose from the marsh and swept regally across the river to the other side, disappearing into the tall grass.

Yes, there was something peaceful about this place, something welcoming. She wished she didn't have to go.

Then she saw him, at the back of the boat, squatting down as he studied something intently. His body, caught by the sun's rays, glowed in a golden hue. He was so sleek and strong, with the graceful moves of some jungle savage. The sight of him brought an odd quiver to her body, and she caught her breath. The tendons in her knees weakened and her blood seemed to stop, refusing to move through her veins. If she hadn't leaned against the galley, she would have swayed.

She must have made a sound, because suddenly he looked up. Their gazes met, and she felt that same powerful feeling arc between them.

"Did you sleep well?"

"Yes. I'm sorry. I guess I'm not as strong as I look."

"You don't look very strong."

"I know. I look dreadful."

He decided she was wrong. She didn't look dreadful. She looked ethereal, delicate. Even in the stiff little skirt and simple blouse, she seemed wrapped in a dreamlike quality that prickled his nerve endings.

She returned his stare for a moment, then said, "It's stopped raining."

"Yes. The water has already started to recede."

"I'll be able to leave tomorrow."

"Perhaps, but not in your car."

"Why?"

"You won't be able to drive it out of the mire. It was too light to withstand the current and it got washed off the road. The same thing might have happened to my truck, if you hadn't forced me to leave it so far back."

Sean knew he probably could have hooked a rope to the car and pulled it back on the road with his truck. But the wet ground might not provide enough traction, and for some reason he was reluctant to try.

"There's more bad news," he went on.

"Oh?" She didn't tell him, but the news that she probably couldn't leave yet didn't dismay her.

"You left your windows open. The flood swept right through the car and took your suitcase with it."

"And probably my purse as well. I must have left it behind." Carolina looked down at her skirt and blouse and frowned. "I suppose it could have been worse. At least I still have this suit."

"I think I liked you better in my shirt."

Sean hadn't meant to say it, but it was true. The skirt made her a real person, not his private dream. Now there was an awkward moment of silence, of awareness, of confusion.

"So did I," she said softly, then added more hurriedly, "What are you doing?"

"I'm preparing my bed for tonight." He lifted the end of a heavy white corded object that looked like some giant crocheted doily. "It's a hammock."

"You're going to sleep out here? Won't the mosquitoes eat you alive?"

"Nope, I have a mosquito net." He attached the hammock to the far mast and walked it forward to hang it on a nail on the back wall of the galley. Next he took a fine, gauzy net and set it up. Suddenly the hammock was covered by a waterfall-like tent of webbing.

"Oh, it's wonderful," Carolina said. "May I try it?"

"Sure, come inside." He lifted the net and made room for her as she slipped inside. "You pull the edge of the hammock out and sit in the middle."

But Carolina was too light and the hemp was too strong. Every time she tried to lie down, the edges simply closed over her as if she were a fish caught inside a net.

"Here, let me sit beside you and hold it open."

Sean sat. That was a mistake. He so outweighed her that she tumbled into his waiting arms as if it had all been planned.

"Whoa!"

They were both snarled in the swinging net.

"I'm sorry," she said, trying to separate herself by twisting in Sean's arms. But the more they struggled, the more entangled they became. Sean's fingers inadvertently found Carolina's ticklish spot. She jerked and began to laugh. It was as if her earlier dream of swinging in a hammock with a lover had come true. Sean was silent for a moment; then, as she began tickling him back, his laughter joined hers.

"All right, already," she heard him say. "You've got me at your mercy. What is this, death by tickling?"

"You started it."

Hands touched, legs grazed. The hammock turned, finally dumping them unceremoniously to the deck, his strong body landing first, cushioning the blow as she landed on top.

"Are you all right?" he asked from his position beneath her, his smile quickly replaced by a scowl.

"I think so. You don't have to be ashamed of having fun. You have a nice laugh, Sean Rogan. I don't think you laugh much."

There was a breathlessness in her voice.

"I don't have much to laugh about."

"But of course you do. You have this wonderful boat, and the freedom to live any way you choose, to be—to be here. You can't know what that means."

Freedom was important to her. He didn't yet know why, but he could understand. And she was right—the boat *was* important, not because it was his, but because it had been wounded and he'd given it life again. There was something wounded about Carolina Evans too.

"You're here too," he said, his eyes searching for something that he couldn't name.

"Yes, I am. What happened to your face?" She couldn't stop her fingertips from tracing the scar that ran from his hairline to his eyebrow and to the corner of his frowning eyes.

"I slipped through a hole on deck and caught a splinter as I fell."

"Did it hurt?"

"Like hell."

"You curse a lot, don't you?"

"I guess you're not used to hearing such language from the men you know."

"No, the men I know are more . . . refined, they'd say. I'd call it more controlled. They don't allow their emotions to show quite so strongly as you do."

"What makes you think I let my emotions show?"

She allowed a playful smile to part her lips. He could see her small pink tongue and white teeth.

"Don't you?" she asked, and gave a wiggle to her body, the body that was pressing against the part of his anatomy that continued to defy his control. "I'd say your emotions are very strong, and very obvious."

With a growl, he came to his feet, bringing her with him. "Stop it, witch, or you're liable to find out how strong I really am."

"I think, Captain Rogan, that I might like discovering the extent of your strength."

He held her arms, pushing her away as he took a deep, calming breath. "No, Carolina. And you'd do well not to tempt me. You don't even know me. I'm not what you think. I'm not some safe haven in the storm. I hurt people; that's why I prefer inanimate objects that don't resist my control."

"'Hurt people'? I think you're the one who's been hurt. Now you're a recluse, Rogan, a rough, quiet man who avoids people. But you're not violent. Ida, the woman at the inn, told me how kind you are, how you contribute money to the town, how much they depend on you."

"I'm just buying my privacy. That's self-defense, not kindness. I can't imagine why Ida told you anything. She knows better." His moment of lightness was gone. "Let's eat, before the stew burns." He deftly turned her around and pushed her toward the galley.

Carolina didn't think she was hungry, but after she tasted the first sip she realized how wrong she was. For the first time in a long time, she relished the food she was eating.

"You know I can't take your bed," she said.

"Well, I suppose you could share it with me."

She studied him carefully. "I think I would, but I don't believe you really mean that."

"You're right, Carolina Evans. So I'm going to sleep on deck. But meanwhile we're going to talk. You know that I'm an honorable hermit with money. I think it's time I knew about you. Tell me your story."

He was right. She owed him the truth. If, after hearing it, he dumped her in the river, it was probably what she deserved. Lord knew she'd thought about jumping in enough times herself.

"All right. As you already know, I've been ill. I was always small, frail, but they never found anything wrong. If I had a cold, it turned into pneumonia. If I skinned my knee, it got infected. I missed a lot of school as a child."

"So, you weren't strong. That happens. Your mother must have worried about you."

"My mother died when I was six. Afterward my father kept me pretty close. If I didn't come in contact with sick children, I might stay healthy, was his philosophy. There were nurses, housekeepers, tutors. It wasn't until I was in high school that I began to seriously question my isolation."

"What was wrong with you?"

"There was nothing wrong. I finally figured it out and forced my father to agree. At last he relented and said that I could attend college, so long as it was the local one and I lived at home. And I did, for over two years. Then I turned rebel. I ran away."

"I can understand that. Nobody wants to be totally controlled. But even I can tell that you aren't very strong."

"No, you don't understand. I rebelled because I didn't believe that I was really sick when I was growing up, no more than any other child. He'd lied to me—out of fear, I think. My mother was a weak woman with many problems, and after she died he thought I should be protected."

"So you grew up and ran away. Why?"

"I wanted to find my own way, make a life for myself. He refused to let me go. But I had my own money, the interest on a trust fund from my mother. I applied to Southern Methodist University, and when I was accepted, I simply packed my bags, wrote a note for my father, and left. The next day he was in Dallas trying to take me home."

"What is your father, a tyrant?"

"No, not really. He's just convinced that he's right, like most attorneys who always win."

"An attorney? Damn! I'm convinced that the worst people on the face of the earth are lawyers."

"Oh? Do you have someone in your family who's an attorney?"

"Yes, me."

It was Carolina's turn to groan. Of all the professions in the world, her sea captain would have to be an attorney, like her father. But that was where the similarities ended. Her father would never be caught dead in a pair of worn shorts on a boat moored in the middle of a marsh. No, their professions might be the same, but that was all.

"Go on," Rogan said, filling their glasses with more ice and sweet tea. "You ran away from home and went to college. What was wrong with that? Did you run off with a guy?"

"No."

"What happened?"

"It was toward the end of my senior year when I got into trouble. I passed out, and my friend called my father, who accused him of not taking care of me—as he'd been paid to do. This time I had to go home."

"Your father paid someone to look after you, and he got you in trouble? No wonder you didn't want to marry him."

Carolina took a big sip of tea as she considered his question. Then she began to laugh. "Marry him? You thought—?" She laughed again, then turned serious. "No, Rogan, this time I really was sick. My passing out started with a seizure. All those years, when Father told me I was too sick to live a normal life, I wasn't. Then, when I finally broke away, all his predictions came true."

"How? What happened?"

He looked at her closely, touching the feathery ends of her short hair, and lifted his eyebrows. "Your head really has been shaved." His fingertips found the scar at the base of her skull and paused.

"No—well, yes, I had surgery. But that wasn't the only reason I lost my hair. They finally found out that I had a kind of tumor, a cyst on my pituitary gland that messed up my thyroid, my hormones, all my controls. First they operated. Then came the radiation therapy."

"And? Are you all right now?" He knew his voice was harsh, that he was ordering her to say she was all right. As he waited, he realized that he had no right to be angry or to care. But he did, and that shocked him.

"They think so, with medication," she whispered. "I'll probably never be more than five feet two inches tall. And if I weigh more than a hundred pounds, I'll be overweight. But otherwise, I'll probably be fine."

"Damn!"

"Damn!" the parrot repeated. Somewhere in the cabin below there was a loud thump, and the ship rocked as if a barrel had rolled from one side of it to the other.

"There it goes again," Sean said, striding out of the galley and into the cabin below. "Poltergeists."

Carolina sat in the galley, the small lamp casting long shadows across the small room. She imagined her great-grandmother six times removed, sitting in the same galley with Jacob. She didn't know how Sean would feel when he learned that over a hundred years earlier, their ancestors must have been lovers. Did that mean she and Rogan were related? Then she decided it didn't matter.

Carolina knew little about the first Carolina because she'd died shortly after her child was born. To their child, Jacob had been a stern, unbending man. The journals had clearly shown him to be dictatorial and possessive—something, she'd decided, like her own father.

"Nothing down there. There never is," Rogan said as he entered the galley once more. "Sounds, movement, tobacco smoke—I don't know."

"Tobacco smoke? Have you given any thought to the possibility that there might be somebody here, watching?"

Everything went still. The ship seemed to pause in mid-rock. Bully hushed. For a moment neither Sean nor Carolina could hear the other breathe.

"There's nobody along this river for ten miles, other than Harry upstream who brings me fish and old Lucy who sends me fried pies. Nobody is watching us, I'm certain!"

This time the boat rocked, and Bully cried out in alarm.

"And furthermore, I think it's time that you told me the real truth. Why are you here?"

"There is no other reason, at least not one I'm sure of, Rogan. During the time I was sick I discovered the journal in my father's library. I became fascinated with it. My father explained that my mother had read the journal and that after learning Carolina was an ancestor, she'd named me for her. I can't explain why I came, but I think maybe it was because I really was sent for."

Sean couldn't conceal his amazement. "You're serious, aren't you?" When she nodded, he asked, "By whom and for what reason?"

"I don't know. Why did you come here? Why did you raise the ship? How did we come to be together, here, in this time? Almost a hundred and fifty years later, Rogan and Carolina together again?"

"I'm not buying that, Goldilocks. You're here, but not for long. I don't know anything about Jacob Rogan and don't want to. The Rogans have spent the best parts of their lives reliving past glories and trying to capture new ones. I put that behind me two years ago. I'm here, and I'm living my life in this minute. I don't have much use for fate. I don't believe in the Ouija board, and fortune-tellers are only for the fanciful who want an excuse for failure. I'll take care of me and my future, and I'll do it alone."

He looked so pained, so desperate. She understood his need for freedom. "I know; I'll be leaving soon. I'm sorry I intruded."

"You're not the complication, Goldilocks. The bad guys are my loving family; and the power players, the politicians, the crooks are the complications. Now I've got the State of Georgia breathing down my back, claiming the *Butterfly*. And you didn't have a thing to do with that."

"I heard you tell Harry about their claim. How can they do that?"

"It seems there is a law about antiquities belonging to the state."

"But the *Scarlet Butterfly* is yours."

"I know, but without a bill of sale I really can't prove it, and there's a law that says any object found in navigable waters legally belongs to the state. And the St. Marys River is navigable."

"But you said this is a lake."

"A saltwater lake, fed by both the river and the Atlantic, which makes it part of Georgia."

"Can't you fight it?"

"Oh, I intend to, but I'm told that I'm not likely to win."

"Oh, Rogan, I'm so sorry. I wish I could help. You're welcome to my records. Carolina's daughter's journal refers to her father, Jacob, and the *Butterfly*."

"You really have a journal that says Jacob Rogan owned the *Scarlet Butterfly*?"

"Not exactly. It just refers to the boat and the captain sailing the *Butterfly*. That ought to mean something." Carolina thought about the journal for a moment and began to smile. "Hey, that has to be the answer—why I'm here. It really is fate. I was meant to come here, to bring you the journal."

Rogan shook his head. He didn't believe in fate. A

man made his own choices and set his own course of action. Like his brother had said, the woman was a fruitcake. Well, not a fruitcake, maybe just a disillusioned child who needed magic in her life. And, he decided, she was leaving the next day. He had to stop her fantasy before it became contagious.

"Oh, Rogan. I just remembered. The journal was in my suitcase."

"And your suitcase is gone. So much for your being my angel of mercy."

"But we can find it. It's red, and it ought to be easily seen."

"That suitcase could be caught in the swamp, the marsh, or have already washed out into the Atlantic. Thanks, but I doubt it would have helped anyway."

"Oh, Rogan, I'm so sorry."

He was sorry too. And if he didn't get his mind on something else, they'd be comforting each other in a way that would not be smart. She was too trusting, and his newly discovered spot of compassion was still clinging desperately to life.

"There is a shower on the side of the galley, if you'd like to take a bath, Carolina. I'll get you something to sleep in. Then I suggest you turn in. Tomorrow we'll go into town and make arrangements to have your car towed."

His voice was gruff again. She'd come to realize that this stern manner appeared anytime his emotions were touched. She understood. She'd found a way or two to hide her own over the years.

"A shower? A real shower?"

"Yes. It's a crude affair, nothing more than a tub of rainwater with a pully release system, but it works.

You clear the table, and I'll set up the tub for you to stand in."

It was a shower, and it was crude. But Carolina washed her hair and her underclothes. Later, dressed in one of Rogan's oversized T-shirts, she felt better than she had in two days.

Rogan was busy in the galley when she came to say good night. He appeared determined not to look at her, and she was glad. The boat seemed small and the space confining. He didn't have to say so for her to know that he was feeling the constriction too.

"Are you sure about the hammock?" she asked.

"I'm sure. I often sleep on deck. It's cooler."

She didn't know how he'd react, but she padded barefoot to his side, instinctively stretched up and kissed him on the cheek.

"Then I won't argue, Captain. I'll just say good night. And thank you for everything. I don't want to be a burden to you. I like you—even if you are a lawyer."

"Carolina?" His voice stopped her at the cabin door. "What did you study in school?"

"Art. I wanted to paint all the beautiful things in the world. Then I found out the world wasn't so beautiful."

"I should have known."

"And, Rogan, I think you ought to know that the first Carolina was an artist too. I realize this will sound unimportant to you, but Jacob didn't want her on board either."

"That's the trouble, Carolina," he said, just under his breath. "I think I do."

• • •

The next morning the dock and the bank beyond were exposed by the receding water. After breakfast, Rogan offered to drive Carolina into town. He seemed preoccupied and cross. Of course she had to go; she'd never called her father. But she didn't want to leave. As if in agreement with her, the soggy ground sucked at her sandals as she walked along behind Rogan.

"We'll stop at Ida's and have a real breakfast," Rogan said. "Then you can pick up something more practical to wear."

"Clothes?" Carolina started.

"You'll need a swimsuit, some shorts, and maybe a bright-colored dress, for a special occasion."

"A special occasion?"

"Well, you never know what fate might have arranged for you, Goldilocks."

It wasn't what fate had arranged that interested her so much as what Rogan was arranging.

The marsh was alive with sound. Birds and insects were in constant movement through the grasses and tree limbs. Here and there, caught in the brush, were the ugly signs of civilization; paper cups, soft-drink cans, and wrappers. Those within reaching distance Rogan retrieved. He'd brought along a plastic bag for that purpose.

"The trappings of civilization," Carolina commented. "I think I like the jungle better. Natural, without refinement."

"Sure, I can tell you'd enjoy living out here without hot water, without restaurants, without a cook."

"Please don't remind me of those eggs," she said brightly. "But I really love it." She did. There was something so free and easy about the boat and the river, though she couldn't expect him to believe she felt this way. "Oh, there's a path. Where does it go?"

"To the house."

"There's a real house out here?"

"What's left of it. Old Jacob must have gotten tired of living on board at some time, or maybe it was his descendants. At any rate, one of the Rogans built a very grand house overlooking the water."

"Can I see it?"

"Not now. It's falling down," he snapped, pressing on down the road. "Besides, we need to get into town."

"Oh, I see." He didn't want to share the house with her, even for a moment. She didn't understand, but she could accept that. So far she'd inserted herself into his life freely, with little regard for his privacy. She'd done more than she'd ever expected to do when she left Texas. She'd found the *Scarlet Butterfly*. And she'd found her Rogan.

My Rogan. There was a nice sound to the words. She hurried to catch up with him. This morning he was wearing crisp khaki trousers and a blue shirt with only a few wrinkles. On his feet were a pair of scruffy running shoes. Once again his hair was pulled neatly back and caught with a rubber band.

With a little imagination she could see him in a captain's navy pea coat, dark-colored trousers, and shoes. He'd be wearing a beard, or possibly just a mustache. He would have—in another life. And her? She couldn't quite get a picture of what she might be wearing; then she realized with a start that it might be because she wasn't there at all.

"There. You can see the problem." His voice broke through her thoughts. She struggled to focus on what he was saying, then caught sight of the red car. It was resting at a crazy angle against a tree in a swampy area about ten feet off the road. "Yes, I can see. It's a good thing that I took insurance on the rental."

"Did you pay for it with a credit card?"

"Yes, it's paid in advance."

"Then you didn't need insurance. That's covered by your card."

"Oh, well, I don't suppose it matters." *I'm* not paying for it, she could have said. All the cards were in her father's name. "At least your truck isn't hurt."

"No, thank goodness for big tires."

They reached the battered black truck farther up the road, and Rogan opened the door. She could see where the waterline fell, just under the edge of the fender. The engine cranked easily, and with great skill Rogan backed up the vehicle until he came to a place where he could turn around and head toward town.

"I wish we could travel on the river," he said. "It's beautiful."

"So do I. But I like the marsh, too, and the moss. It's so lush and green, so different from Houston where I grew up. Is St. Marys very old?"

"Dating back to Oglethorpe and the first settlers, somewhere around 1733."

"Did a Rogan come along with Oglethorpe?"

"Probably not. They claim to have migrated to Georgia from Charleston, but my guess is that they were residing in some English prison when they accepted the invitation to come here."

Maybe it was Sean's imagination, but Carolina's face seemed to have more color in it this morning. Or maybe it was just the light of interest in her eyes. If he could get her out of that prim white blouse, he reflected, and into some bright clothes, she'd look . . . beautiful and alive.

That thought sent a jab of sensation down his leg from the point where they touched, and he inadvertently gave the truck a spurt of gas before he turned his mind to the question she was asking.

"What on earth did the early settlers do here? I can't see them growing cotton on this land, and I thought cotton was king."

"They grew cotton farther inland. Along the river it was rice. And timber. There were plenty of vessels sailing upriver from the town of St. Marys then. But St. Marys is the only one of the river towns to survive."

Sean drove slowly as they came into town, following the main street until it dead-ended into the docks by the river.

There were shrimp boats and pleasure craft anchored at the docks. She could see warehouses and, farther down, a small ferryboat.

"That's the *Cumberland Queen*," Sean said. "It takes visitors over to Cumberland Island. Shall we shop first, or go to Ida's for breakfast?"

"Shop," she said, "if you're not too hungry. Then maybe an early lunch. Oh! Oh, dear!"

"What's wrong?"

When they'd started out, Carolina hadn't considered precisely what buying new clothes would mean. Now it occurred to her that not only had her suitcase washed away, but so had her purse, with her credit cards and her money.

"I'm afraid that I have a small problem, Rogan: I

have no money. Remember, my purse was in the car." What she had chosen to ignore was that her medication was also in the purse. Having the prescription refilled would mean contacting her doctor, and that would give her location away. Going without medication for a few days would probably do her no great damage, for the thyroid replacement lasted for as long as thirty days. Still, she'd have to make arrangements to get more medication soon or run a real risk of unpleasant side effects.

But not yet. She'd take a chance. Staying with Rogan for a few days was worth it.

Rogan drummed his fingers against the center of the steering wheel. "Tell you what: I'll be glad to make you a loan. Where would you like to go to shop?"

"Well, Ida told me there was a warehouse that has been converted into small shops and boutiques. Have you been there?"

"Nope. The hardware store and the grocery store are the extent of my shopping excursions here. But I think I know the building."

It soon became apparent that while Rogan professed to no great knowledge of shopping, he had a keen eye for women's clothing. She'd never been shopping with anyone who let her make her own choices. Still, his enthusiasm was hard to resist, and when they were done she'd followed his wishes almost completely.

Finally, Rogan left Carolina as she was changing in to one of her new dresses. He returned shortly carrying a parcel of his own. Carolina was wearing a bright blue sundress with matching shoes. She looked like sunshine, and a smile of approval replaced Rogan's customary frown.

They walked back along the docks, listening to the squawking gulls, watching the tourists snapping pictures, and buying souvenirs. Rogan bought her a pair of funky earrings that clamped on the side of her ear and sounded like musical bells when she moved her head. Time passed so pleasantly that she protested when Rogan said that it was lunchtime and she needed to rest. They headed back to the truck and Ridgeway Inn, where Ida welcomed them warmly.

"Come inside. Carolina, I was worried about you when that storm blew in and you didn't come back. Then Harry turned up and said you were with Rogan. And you"—she hugged Rogan and gave him a sharp look—"are you behaving yourself?"

"After the glowing lies you gave Carolina about my character, why would you ask such a question, Ida?"

"Because I've seen the wild beast hidden in those eyes, and you weren't expecting Beauty here to drop in. I'm glad to see you're getting along. I wasn't sure that the sheriff hadn't arrested you."

"Oh, you heard about the boat?"

"Boat? No. I heard about Carolina's father. He's burning up the telephone lines between here and Texas."

"Father? How did he find me? I intended to call him, but the storm isolated us and Mr. Rogan didn't have a phone. He didn't know where I was going. I even bought my ticket under an assumed name."

Rogan thought for a minute, then turned his gaze to face Carolina. "How'd you pay for the ticket, Goldilocks?"

"With cash. I didn't want him to trace me too quickly."

"And the rental car?"

"Oh, no. The charge card. They wouldn't let me take it without a charge card number. Now he'll come after me."

"So? You're old enough to make your own decisions. If you don't want to go home, tell him."

"I will. Right after lunch," she added with more confidence. "I'll call him. Right now, I'm starved."

Ida showed them to a table overlooking the river. "Just sit right here and enjoy the sunshine. You look like you could use some, and some good food too. I'll bring it."

They sat for a long time, just watching the dark water flowing by the open veranda. Between the porch and the water was a gentle slope that showed the evidence of a rising river's ravages.

"It's so peaceful here, Rogan. I can understand why Jacob and Carolina came here."

"You're such a romantic, Goldilocks, such an optimist."

"And you, Rogan, what are you? Why'd you turn your back on your family?"

"Who told you about my family?"

"Nobody, at least nobody but you. Your brother refused to tell me anything more than what was in the article. It said that your family has been in south Georgia for a hundred years. They once owned most of this corner of the state. Before the War Between the States they were into farming and shipping. Do you really own newspapers and television stations?"

"Not anymore. All I own is one 1850's schooner

and a hundred acres on the river. The rest belongs to two brothers and three sisters."

"But the article said your family is worth millions."

"Yep. Although we've tried our damnedest to lose it over the years, it kept on expanding."

"You were the chairman of the board. And you just walked away?"

"Wrong. I didn't walk. I ran, as hard as I could."

"Why would you do that? Don't you care about your family?"

"Let's just say that it's better if I leave them all alone. They like it that way, and so do I."

"But what will you do with the rest of your life?"

"Just what I've been doing—nothing. Why does a person have to do something? I'm restoring my boat. When I'm finished, I'll start on the house. I like working with my hands, by myself, without anybody to answer to or have to explain to."

Carolina was surprised at his honesty, and touched. His show of indifference was convincing, but not totally. What had happened to make this strong man walk away from his responsibilities? Why did he hurt? And why was she so tuned in to his pain?

"But don't you get lonely?"

"Sure. That's why I bought the bird."

"A bird isn't exactly what I meant."

"Oh, you mean a woman. That hasn't been a problem. Up to now." He paused as their food arrived. "Up to now, Ida has satisfied all my physical needs, haven't you, darling?" He took the plate she held and gave her a big wink.

"Watch it, Sean. If Harry hears you say that, you're liable to be in big trouble. You know how jealous he gets."

Carolina recalled the frail-looking old man in the boat and looked at Rogan. She remembered an old musical with Frank Sinatra. He'd sung a song about an ant who had high hopes about felling a huge rubber tree plant. She smiled.

"That isn't exactly what I meant, Rogan. I've been by myself, and it's lonely. There's a whole world out there. Don't you even want to see it?"

"One hotel room is pretty much like another. I guess I've never spent much time looking. I gave up on new places—and I like it here. I like knowing that tomorrow morning I'll wake up on my boat, look out and see the same shoreline, hear the same sounds, and do whatever I choose. There's a whole world out there all right, and you're welcome to it. The world will swallow you up if you're not careful."

"Sometimes staying in one place can destroy you too."

"I hope not, because I don't ever intend to leave."

"I suppose everyone has different needs," Carolina said softly. "I'm sorry that you've been treated badly."

"Me? Hell, I'm not the one running around with a shaved head and hiding from her father."

"No, your hair is very long, but you're hiding from your family. Maybe we're not so different."

They didn't talk for a while as they concentrated on their food. There were bowls of thick homemade vegetable soup and buttered corn bread, followed by a crusty little square pastry filled with shrimp and smothered in a piquant sauce. They drank more sweet iced tea with the meal. Piping chicory coffee and apple pie came afterward.

"Wow. If Ida feeds you like that all the time, I can

see why you're so big." Carolina pushed the dessert plate back and laid her fork across the edge.

Rogan simply looked at her, all pretense at conversation eliminated by the intensity of his gaze. With his napkin, he reached out to wipe a sliver of pie crust from her upper lip. But the napkin fell to the table, and it was his finger that rimmed her lip, setting off a shiver that traveled from her mouth to his hand and up his arm.

"What—what are you going to do now, Goldilocks?"

"I don't know. I'm not going back to Houston. I've spent as much time being sick as I intend to. I have to find a place where I can decide what I want to do with the rest of my life."

"What about St. Marys? The people here are wonderful. They'll take you in and make you one of them and not ask a thing in return. My brother the doctor has an office here. I don't much like him as a relative, but as a doctor, he's top of the line."

"I do like it here. I may look around. But first I ought to call a garage to pull the car out of the marsh. I don't even know if it can still be driven."

"I doubt that it can. There's a branch of that rental company here in town. We'll call them before we go back."

She thought she nodded her agreement, but she couldn't be sure. His fingertips were still resting on her face, cupping her chin possessively, as if he intended to lean forward and whisper in her ear.

"Thank you," she said, "but I can't impose on your hospitality any longer. I mean I wanted to see the *Butterfly*, and I have. But I think I'll see about finding a place in town to stay."

"I don't make an offer unless I mean it, Goldilocks. I'd like to you to stay."

She gazed at him, stunned. "You would? Then I'll accept. Thank you."

He hadn't intended to say that. He'd been trying to come up with ways to get her off the boat and out of his life. But the invitation had just popped out, and he realized with surprise that he meant it. Having Carolina on the *Butterfly* might not be fate, as she believed, but it was nice, very nice.

There was a commotion inside the inn, and voices; then loud steps across the polished wood floor. "There you are, Carolina. Are you all right?"

A tall, foreboding man reached the table, caught Sean's hand, and jerked it away from Carolina's face.

"Father," she said with a gasp, feeling her heart shrivel up inside. "What are you doing here?"

Five

"I've come to take you home, Carolina."

"Why?"

"What did you expect me to do, child? After nearly dying, you check yourself out of your doctor's care, pack up your clothes, and run away—just like—"

He didn't complete the sentence, but Carolina knew what he was thinking. Just like her mother.

"I was worried." His face was drawn into a mask of fury that covered his great pain, the mask that served him so well in court. Carolina had a moment of doubt, until he turned toward Sean.

"I'm Angus Evans. Are you responsible for this *stupidity*?"

Under other circumstances, Sean might have tried to explain the situation to the man. He might even have understood how worry could be misinterpreted as anger—until he caught sight of the anguish on Carolina's face. *Stupidity*? What kind of father called his daughter stupid?

"No," she whispered woodenly, "he isn't."

"Yes," Rogan said sharply at the same time, "I am."

"Well, it seems we have a difference of opinion here."

"Carolina is here, with me, and she's fine . . . Mr. Evans, is it? I'm Sean Rogan. Would you care to sit down and talk about this calmly?"

Carolina stared at Rogan in amazement. What was the man doing? He didn't understand the risk. Her father had been known to ruin an enemy without blinking an eye. He had powerful friends not only in Texas, but all over the world.

"No, Sean." She shook her head. "You don't understand. I don't want you hurt."

"I don't intend to get hurt."

"Smart move, Rogan," Angus Evans said. "Now, Carolina. I don't approve of what you did, but I can understand your need to get away. I have a car waiting outside. If you're determined to go away, I'll arrange a trip for you that will be safe. Please?"

Carolina felt her resolve begin to crumble as it had so many times before. She might not have been able to stand up to her father for herself, but she couldn't allow Rogan to be treated this way. She rose, leaning on the table for support.

"I appreciate your concern, Father, but Mr. Rogan is only trying to be kind to me. I won't have you punish him on my account—not if you ever expect me to come home again."

Angus Evans's eyes widened in surprise.

"I do have some money of my own, and I intend to work."

"But, Carolina, you aren't ready. The doctor said that it would take months of monitoring before he can be certain of your condition. Please, let me take you home."

"No. I'm sure there are doctors here, Father."

"There is at least one very fine doctor, Mr. Evans," Rogan said quietly. "Carolina isn't going anywhere, except with me. I'll take care of her." Rogan moved around the table. "Are you finished here, darling?"

Carolina couldn't believe it when Rogan pulled her close and slid his arm around her. "I appreciate your concern for Carolina," he said, "but you don't need to worry. She'll be fine. Now, you'll have to excuse us. We have to be getting back."

Before Carolina knew what was happening, she and Rogan were leaving. Ida held open the front door and said under her breath, "Quick, you two, before he comes out of shock."

They hadn't reached the truck before he caught up. "All right, Carolina. But you tell this long-haired renegade here that I'm not financing the two of you. What your mother left is in trust. So if he's determined to keep you, he's responsible for you and all your future medical bills. My plane is at the St. Marys airport. I'll wait until four o'clock."

Rogan lifted her into the truck and closed the door. "Thank you, Mr. Evans, but she won't be coming."

Angus Evans stared at Rogan for a long, puzzled moment, then reached inside his coat pocket. "Rogan, take my card. If she needs me, let me know."

Sean took the card and put it in his wallet. He started the engine and drove away, one hand on the wheel, the other a clenched fist.

"How can he talk to you like that?"

"He doesn't mean to sound so cold, Rogan. You don't understand."

"No, I don't. You're his child. Doesn't he care?"

Carolina felt a stirring of pain. "No, I'm not his child. And he knows it. I'm his responsibility, but not his child."

"Not his child? What do you mean?"

"My mother made his life hell. There were times when she was all right—sober—and she'd be sorry. She'd promise never to be '*bad*' again, and he'd forgive her. Then the next day she'd be gone once more. The last time he found her she was pregnant with me."

"So why does he want you back?"

"I was my mother's child. He could never stop her, but he's spent his life protecting me, making certain that I don't turn out—'*bad*'."

"So who is this man, the head of the Texas Mafia?"

"No—at least I don't think so—but he's got about as much power. He's just a very lonely man. But he can ruin you, if he chooses."

"Not me. I don't have anything to lose, except my boat, and it looks as if I'm going to do that all by myself."

Rogan drove, not speaking, lost in his thoughts, thoughts that swam and veered, just as they'd done so often when he'd dealt with *his* family. Why hadn't he let Carolina and her father work out their differences? He didn't want to take on her problems. He didn't want to take on Carolina.

"Rogan? Rogan! I appreciate your playing my knight in shining armor, but the truth is, I'm no stray kitten to be adopted until you can find it a home."

"What?" He was turning off the highway and onto the dirt road that led to the river.

"I think you'd better turn around and take me back."

"I probably should. Do you want to go?"

"Of course not, Rogan. But what do you plan to do with me, now that you've slain my dragon?"

"'Do' with you?" He focused his attention on the woman sitting beside him, trying to stop the fierce need from igniting within him. Her eyes were wide. They'd turned that silvery color that announced her uncertainty, that reached out and fanned the little spot of heat in the pit of his stomach that seemed never to die completely.

"Yes. You've angered my father. He says he's dumping me on you, and you've driven off into the sunset without thinking about what that could mean. What do you intend to do with me?" She tried not to reveal the depth of her turmoil as she waited for his answer.

"'Do'? That's simple. You're going to help me finish restoring the schooner. You're going to learn to cook. And you're going to paint the *Butterfly*'s portrait before they take her away."

"But—Rogan—" She was too stunned to think straight. "I'd be honored to paint the *Scarlet Butterfly*. I'd love to learn to cook, and I'm more than willing to become an apprentice carpenter, but I warn you, I'm a klutz. Oh, Rogan, I don't have any paints."

"Yes you do. I bought them." From behind the seat he lifted the bag he'd put in the truck, and handed it to her. "I figured that you needed something to occupy your hands, so you'd keep them off me."

Inside she found canvases, oil paints, charcoal, brushes. Everything she'd need. She was touched by his thoughtfulness. She hadn't expected it. First the earrings, now this.

Her father had cared for her, providing the things he thought she ought to have. But Sean was the first man she'd ever known who did something for her simply because he knew it would give her pleasure. This from a man who was a tough-talking bad guy.

She took in a light breath, tearing her gaze away from his strong face, now furrowed in a scowl. She was uncertain how to answer. "Are you really offering me a job?"

"A job?" He hadn't thought of it quite that way, but it made some kind of sense. "Yes, I guess I am. The pay is lousy, but the room and board ought to be right up your alley."

"And where do you expect me to live?"

"Right here, Goldilocks. Right here with me."

"Oh, Rogan, thank you." Impulsively, she slid across the seat, tucked an errant strand of hair behind his ear, and planted a kiss on his cheek. "I very much want to be here with you."

"Damn!" Rogan gulped in a breath of air, parked the truck, and pulled her into his arms with a growl of frustration. He'd fought the urge all day and he couldn't stop himself any longer. He wanted just to hold her, nothing more. Just to give her a simple hug that signified their agreement.

She stiffened for a moment, then melted against him. "You know, I rather thought you wanted to hit me," she said.

"Did your father ever do that?"

"Of course not. I know he loved me, but he never got that close. He pushed me away too."

"Too?" Rogan pulled back and looked down at her.

"Does this look like I'm pushing? The Galahad half of me wants to let you go but the rogue wants to make love to you."

"I don't know much about Galahads," she whispered, "but I think I like this rogue. Why is he holding back?"

"Because you aren't ready. You've just escaped from your father, who was a tyrant, and you've mixed me up in your mind with some fantasy sea captain."

"And aren't you the captain of your ship?"

"I don't know what I am, Carolina Evans, and I intend to go very slowly until we both know."

"Will you kiss me, Rogan?"

"Dammit, I shouldn't. I won't." But she looked up at him with such simple trust, such need, that he couldn't resist.

"Where'd the river get its name?"

They were sitting on deck, drinking lemonade and watching the sun set as fireflies twinkled in the darkness. A strong spraying of insecticide kept unwanted night creatures away.

"According to Ida, it came from the sixteenth-century Spanish mission of Santa Maria de Guadeloupe. There's still an old building called the Sugar House where the mission is supposed to have stood. I've never been there. But Santa Maria apparently became Americanized to St. Marys.

There was a stillness about the night that seemed to capture them in its magic. After sharing one kiss in the truck, they'd come on board and, in unspoken agreement, put the conflict with her father aside.

They'd eaten the fried pies, still warm from the pan. "Lucy," Sean had explained, "makes them from dried apricots." Then he'd cleaned the two catfish that were hanging from a thong in the water. Later he'd showed her how to roll them in beaten eggs and cornmeal and had delighted in her pleasure over her success in frying them to a golden crisp.

"The fish are from Harry. Every time he goes into town he leaves fish and pies."

"What about the peaches?" she asked later as they peeled and ate the sweet fruit.

"Now that's a puzzle," he admitted. "So far as I know neither Lucy nor Harry has a tree."

"I like peaches. They're my favorite fruit."

"Peaches for Carrie," Bully said seriously. "Sweets for the sweet."

Rogan looked at Bully with a frown. The bird usually repeated phrases he'd heard, over and over again. His newfound vocabulary was puzzling. *Peaches for Carrie?*

"Why don't you ever talk to the bird?" Carolina asked.

"I don't know. Feel foolish, I guess. There are times I tell him to shut up, but that doesn't stop him."

"Isn't there anything you miss, being so isolated?"

"I guess the only thing I miss is ice cream, and someone to be with occasionally."

"'Be with'? Rogan?" He could have said shared the chores with, or talk with, but *be with?* She hadn't thought about being intimate with him. But Rogan had every right to think that when she said yes to living with him, she'd meant that she was willing to share his bed. And for a moment, that thought sent her nerve endings spiraling. "I didn't think . . . I mean I'm not—"

"Relax. I know. That's all right. I was only teasing."

"Rogan teasing? That seems illogical."

Rogan cleared his throat as if he were embarrassed, and turned away.

Suddenly Rogan's thoughts, and he suspected Carolina's as well, were thrust back to that first night on board. Neither looked at the other. Neither voiced any reflections.

What had he expected? That was the problem, he told himself. He hadn't thought ahead. For the first time, Mr. Bottom-Line-Planner hadn't considered the future. The man who'd always considered all the alternatives hadn't calculated the final result. He was flying by the seat of his pants, and that was new. So new that he didn't know what he'd want to happen even if he could set the terms.

"Well," Rogan said, letting out a deep sigh, "I guess it's time to put up my mosquito netting."

"Rogan, I think you ought to let me sleep up here. I don't feel right about keeping you out of your bed."

"We could always share it," he said quietly.

"We could," she agreed in a soft voice.

"Carolina, are you a virgin?"

His question caught her by surprise. She didn't know quite how to answer. "No . . . or perhaps yes. I'm not really sure."

Rogan stopped unwrapping his netting. "You're not sure? How can that be?"

"It's hard to talk about. When I went away to school, my father was very concerned that I'd do something even more foolish. As I alluded to before, he arranged for me to meet someone. The man—no;

'boy' would be a better word—wasn't really interested. So we never—I mean he tried, but it was just like my father said: I'm not sexually appealing as a woman. I understand and accept that." She turned away, unable to finish, so great was her mortification.

"'Not appealing'?" He dropped the netting and caught her hand, lifting her from her chair, pulling her closer. "You aren't appealing as a woman? The boy must have been an android. Surely you know how truly sensual you are?"

"Me? 'Sensual'? Don't tease me, Rogan. I've learned to live with the truth."

"Listen, Goldilocks, if I weren't holding on with every ounce of control, I'd already have you down in that bed doing things to you that your father would keelhaul me for."

"Thank you for trying to make me feel better, but you don't have to say that. I know how I look. I never did have much in the way of curves. Now I'm a mess."

It was those eyes that did it, those wide, hurting, silver-blue eyes. She really didn't know how appealing she was. Damn Angus Evans for making her feel inferior. Rogan couldn't stand there and allow her to hurt.

He didn't give himself time to consider the problem any further. Acting on instinct, he moved closer to her, his free hand touching her face, his fingertips drawing little stars across her forehead, sliding down to her chin, and lifting it so that she had to look at him.

"You are so lovely, so very special, Carolina," he said softly. "You're like a rare piece of music, a fine painting, an exquisite glass sculpture." He knew, though, that it wasn't a *thing* she needed to be, but a woman, a woman desired, a woman who believed in herself.

Then his lips captured hers, gently, slowly, his hand sliding down her cheek, cupping her shoulder, setting off spears of hot feelings, wondrous little bubbles of sensation that burst across her bare shoulders. He nibbled, tasted, pulling a lip into his mouth, releasing it and finding a new place for his mouth to explore while his hands ranged lower.

He loosened her straps, sliding the top of her sundress to her waist while he found her breasts and brought such sensation to them that she gasped. She began to ache, a surge of unexpected flame licking out in a widening circle from where she felt his throbbing against her. "Oh!"

He pulled back. "What's wrong? Did I scare you?"

"No. I just felt you, against me, like before. Foreplay," she said dreamily, and closed her eyes in contentment.

"Darling, that's just the beginning. If this turns you on, I can't wait until we get to the real thing."

"Oh, yes. Is it all right to talk about it? I mean do women—am I supposed to keep quiet and still?"

"Hell, I hope not. What you do is let go, Carolina, and feel what I'm giving you."

Sean had made love to many women in his life, but never had the loving given him such pleasure. For every caress, she responded with sighs, moans, soft happy little sounds and movements that made him yearn to give her more. If he'd stopped to think, he might have wondered about tomorrow, but nothing seemed important beyond the now, beyond the moment when this lovely woman learned how desirable she was.

Finally her dress fell in a cloud around her feet. His shirt and trousers soon joined it.

"May I touch you, Rogan?"

"You'd better not. I might not be able to hold on if you do."

Her body was so unused to such feelings that she didn't question her lack of fear. Her arms went around his neck, encircling his head. She waited for him to pull back, jerk away, or groan in frustration. But it didn't happen. She pressed her lips against him and felt the pressure building, measured by the stiffness of the muscles in his arms.

"Do you really want to make love to me, Rogan?"

"Yes," he admitted harshly. And Rogan understood in that moment that what he was feeling wasn't simply some magnanimous act of kindness toward her. It was for himself as well, for a man who was parched from the unanswered need for kindness, for caring, for gentleness. She'd been right all along! They were meant to be together. Whether it was an accident or some quirk of fate that had brought her into his life, she was here and she was offering herself to him. And he wanted her very much. He ran his fingers up and down her back, feeling the little muscle tremors where he touched her.

There was no restraint in her response, no holding back, no question. It was as if she knew instinctively that they were meant to love each other, and she trusted him enough to follow wherever he led her.

Trust—that was what she was giving. The idea

blew him away. Trust had never before entered into a relationship for Rogan. But then, he'd never found a woman like Carolina Evans before. He wasn't sure he deserved what she was offering.

"Love 'em and leave 'em, darling," Bully squawked.

"Shut up, Bully," Carolina said quietly. "Rogan isn't like that. People who love each other don't leave."

"'Love'?" Rogan stopped. For a long moment he stood absolutely still; then he pushed her away.

"What's wrong, Rogan?"

"Nothing. No, everything. The bird is right, Carolina. People do love each other and leave. People hurt other people in the name of love. Whatever we have here can't be love. It's just two people wanting to give each other pleasure, nothing more. No commitments, no talk of love."

She wasn't sure she believed him, until she saw his grim look and recognized the tension in his body. He was wrong. She knew he was wrong. But she didn't know how to tell him yet. He'd have to find it out for himself.

"Dear Rogan, I stopped planning on forever. Nobody can promise that. I'm not sure I want to talk about commitments either. As for love, I probably wouldn't know love if it bit me on the foot." She laughed lightly. "Hey, lighten up. This is your hired hand speaking, reporting for orders, Captain Rogan, sir."

They stared at each other, both struggling to find their way back into the passion that still simmered.

"You told me I was desirable, Rogan. I very much need to feel desired. Please, tell me again."

"I'm not sure that's wise, Carolina. I think you

need me, and need is addictive. You're very special, and I wouldn't want to hurt you."

"Rogan, you're crazy! I may not have the experience you have, but I know that refusing to give yourself to me won't take away my wanting you. Once want is acknowledged it doesn't go away, does it?"

"Yes, eventually. But sometimes it takes a long time."

"Time? Maybe time doesn't matter. Maybe it's the now that's important to me."

Rogan tightened the muscles in his arms, pulling her close. "I thought you said that you were cured."

"The jury is still out, but they think so. Sometimes it takes a long time to know. Suppose they're wrong. I think I don't want to wait and see." She extended her hand. "So if you really don't mind making love to a bony woman with no curves and no hair, I'd like you to, Rogan. I'd like that very much."

She took his hand and led him down the steps to the cabin. It didn't matter that it was still light, that the bird squawked his disapproval, that the boat rolled and creaked as if a one-legged man were tap-dancing on the deck.

All Carolina's reservations vanished when Rogan took her hand. She ached for this man with a yearning that went beyond any daydream or fantasy. Once she reached the bed, she stood hesitantly. She felt Rogan's gaze on her, bathing her bare upper body in steady warmth. Removing her hand from his, she slid her panties down and kicked them across the floor. Then she did the same for his underwear.

At her touch Rogan felt his pulse quicken to a dangerous rate. He'd meant to give to Carolina, but she was giving to him. She'd found the courage to know what she wanted and to ask for it. There was no uncertainty, but rather a kind of proud confidence.

Rogan reached out, his fingertips touching her breast. He was rewarded with a soft moan and the visible puckering of the nipple.

"Oh, Rogan, that's so nice. May I touch you too?"

"Not yet, darling. There's time for that later." He took her entire breast into his mouth and kissed it, softly.

Her head fell back and her eyes closed as she caught his arms and leaned away so that he could take what he wanted. His kisses felt like butterfly wings brushing against her breasts. She was glowing. All those years of loneliness and want dissolved away. Instinctively she pressed against Rogan and felt him stiffen in response.

She could feel her breasts swell. They weren't small anymore. Rogan had made them beautiful. Like satin, she moved sensually against every part of him she could touch. She felt the roughness of his carpenter's hands on her breasts, his body hair gently caressing her stomach, his maleness caught between them. "I didn't know," she whispered. "I never understood."

This time it was Rogan who groaned. He was losing himself. His heartbeat thundered in his ears and his throat muscles were so tight that he could hardly draw air into his lungs. "Carolina, are you sure?" His voice was so ragged that he didn't recognize it. He'd had to force himself to ask.

"I've never been so certain of anything," she whispered, and felt the fire sweep through him in reply. "I hurt. I feel like every part of me is moving. I want you to make love to me, Rogan. Please? Now?"

And then she was in his arms. He was falling down across the bed holding her, kissing her wildly, touching her with such pleasure that she could no longer doubt his desire. With his dark hair loosened from its perpetual band, it fell across his forehead, skimming her body, setting off ripples of pleasure. She reached out, running her fingers through its luxuriant length, reveling in the sensual feeling, and holding him against her body.

Rogan's mouth explored her breasts, ricocheted to the sensitive area of her neck and downward, leaving patches of fire wherever he touched. He knew when to be gentle and where to exert pressure, as if he'd memorized her body and could predict her responses. Ignoring the frantic hands tugging at him, urging him to move faster, he slid his leg across her, freeing himself to pulsate against her thigh. She responded in rhythm as his mouth left her breasts and ranged lower.

"Not so fast, darling," he said. "I want this to be good for you."

"Rogan, if it were any better, I'd die. Don't torture me, please!"

But she hadn't yet known the exquisite torture of a man's loving until his mouth moved lower, capturing the bead of throbbing heat that jerked wildly at his touch.

"Oh, Rogan, stop. You're going to make me—make me do something!" Her words and her actions were in fierce disagreement as she arched against him, trembling, panting, asking.

But he was trembling, too, now. "That's what I'm trying to do, darling. Go with the feeling, Goldilocks." His fingers moved along the inner part of her thigh, then upward, until he found the spot where his mouth had been. He had to tighten his own muscles to hold back the growing tide of response. Not yet, Rogan. You can't let go yet. His finger drifted lower. Then it was inside her, as far as he could go—so far, but no farther. Stunned, he pulled back and stared at her in wonder.

She *was* a virgin.

Then he felt her response, the slow, subtle beginning of a body ready to soar. But there was to be nothing subtle about Carolina's passion, or her need.

He tried to hold back, to think, to tell himself that he was losing control. But his mind whirled in a storm of desire. And then he was inside her, surrounded by tight heat and moisture, pushing against the barrier and holding back while he tried to allow her body time to adjust.

Every part of his mind was in tune with his desire in a way that he'd never experienced before. Carolina was more than desire, more than sex, more than a vessel for release; she was none of the women he'd ever made love to and yet she was all the women he'd ever wanted. And then he was past the barrier.

If there was pain, she didn't feel it. There was wonder, the beginning of a ripple that increased by the second, turning into a force that was frightening in its intensity. Her little screams had turned into a breathless moan that built and built and exploded into something that she couldn't begin to comprehend.

Sean was stunned by the enormity of what they shared. He fell against her, still joined to her, still feeling little aftershocks, shuddering one last time as he let out a ragged breath.

For a long time he just lay there, supporting his weight on his arms, reluctant to pull himself away.

"Damn!" He rolled over and slapped the side of the bed. "Do you realize what I've done to you, Carolina Evans?"

"Not entirely, but I'm sure I will after I get a little more experience."

"No, I mean I didn't protect you."

"'Protect' me?"

"Babies, darling; that's what happens when you make love without protection. I don't suppose you're taking birth control, are you?"

"Oh, that. No, I'm not taking anything. But you don't have to worry. My doctors have already told me that I'll never conceive. Too much medication, too much radiation. One side effect is that women don't conceive."

"Are you sure?"

"I'm sure."

What the doctor had really said was that it was most unlikely. And that if she did conceive, she wouldn't be able to carry a child to term. At the time that had been the least of her concerns, but now, basking in the warmth of what she'd just shared, she allowed herself to regret her inability to conceive.

Loving Rogan was only a temporary moment in her life. She understood that. He was the now, not the forever. She'd stay as long as he wanted her, then she'd go. She didn't dare plan for more. The thought of a future that included a child was incomprehensible. All she'd ever hoped for was this. She'd stay in his arms for as long as he'd hold her. And nothing would stop her from loving it.

And loving him.

"Is this wonderful feeling going to last, Rogan?" She felt a wave of new longing sweep through her, and she reached out, just to touch his hair, to convince herself that it had been real.

"I don't know. Once I might have said that it was great, and maybe we might try it again sometime. But hell's bells, you've still got me floating in some kind of magnetic field."

"I have? How can you tell?"

"Well, for one thing, I'm already hard again."

"You are? Good." There was a satisfied whisper in her voice, a wonder that she gave reality to as she reached down and touched him. He throbbed beneath her touch, hot and moist and velvety.

"How long can you stay like this?"

"Good question. Normally I'm good for about fifteen minutes, maybe longer, if you don't do anything to hasten the process."

"You're good for fifteen minutes and after that you're bad? I think I want to know about the bad."

"Carolina, another few minutes of your touching me, and you're never going to find out about the bad. I won't last that long." He jerked her hand away, pulling it to his lips, where he planted a kiss in her palm.

"Is there a name for this, for what I feel now?"

"It's called afterglow."

"'Afterglow.' I like that. I feel as if I'm glowing. Are you glowing too?"

"I went past glowing when you touched me. I'm churning. I'm boiling. I'm just plain hurting, darling."

"Oh, Rogan, I never want you to hurt. What can I do to help?"

He moved over her again, studying her beautiful eyes in the shadows. They were a deep blue now, clear and trusting. She smiled as her body closed around him, taking him inside her, slowly and without hesitation.

"Am I hurting you?" she asked.

"Oh, yes, it hurts wonderfully. I like the thought of us taking away each other's hurts." She slid her legs around him, holding him inside her. Her lower body began to vibrate, and he felt the beginning of his own tremors. His mouth found hers, his tongue plunging inside her.

Rogan clutched her shoulders, moaning softly as she arched against him, meeting every thrust with growing tension. He heard her short gasps of pleasure and felt the coil of tension begin to unravel in a shattering heat that caught and built to a crescendo of feeling.

"Oh, Rogan," she whispered. "I never knew."

"Now you do, Carolina," he said as he turned over, pulling her with him so that she was tucked into the space over his heart. "And so do I."

Outside the ship, the water stilled. The sun slid behind the trees and the marsh came to life with the movement of night creatures.

He watched her sleep, watched and thought about another Carrie who might have loved her captain in that same bed. He thought about other golden hair across the pillow, someone else's innocent trust, two other people's growing love. Even the memory was confusing. He didn't know where it had come from or why.

But he felt pain.

Six

Carolina woke to gentle movement and silence. She lay there, eyes closed, allowing the wonderful memories to settle comfortably around her.

She moved gingerly, expecting to feel different, and she was rewarded with a heavy, satisfied fullness. Her legs felt languid, not with the unfocused emptiness that she'd felt for so long, but as if there was a resonant singing in her veins, resting, waiting to surge back to life.

"Now you've done it, Carrie."

Glorying in the sound of his voice, she didn't open her eyes. Instead she stretched, twisting wantonly under his gaze as she felt the sheet slide down to her waist.

"Oh, yes, Rogan. I've finally done it, and magnificently. I think being bad is just about the closest thing to heaven a body can feel."

"Or hell."

"Why don't you come back to bed, Rogan? I'd like that."

"*Not again, Carrie. I'll not allow this to happen again.*"

"But you brought me here."

"*I know, and I can't seem to go back and change anything. But it's wrong. No good can come of this. I learned that lesson well.*"

Carolina felt a sudden coldness sweep across her. "Why are you acting this way, Rogan? This was meant to be."

"*Aye, sweet Carrie. It seems so. And I curse the fates that intervened. I made a promise once, a promise I couldn't keep. Perhaps I've been given a second chance.*"

Carolina felt a brush of coolness across her lips and a quick little breath of air. The silence that followed was colder than any hospital ward during the hours before dawn.

Carolina sat up. "Rogan?"

But he was gone, along with the afterglow that had cushioned her waking.

She came to her feet. Despite buying all those things the day before, they'd forgotten a robe. Suddenly she felt a great urgency to go topside. Grabbing the sheet from the bed, she tucked it around her and climbed the stairs. The sunlight was so bright that she was blinded for a moment. Then she saw him, swimming in the lake, his strong arms reaching for the water and pulling it behind him in a sleek show of fury.

She sat at the edge of the vessel, swinging her feet over the side, and watched. The sun was warm, the day unfolding like a precious blossom for someone who'd never before seen a flower.

Brilliant blue and black dragonflies hovered just over the water, dancing like the prickles of light behind her lids when she closed her eyes. Rogan was working off his uncertainties in the lake, which was clearly defined now that the water level had dropped. Carolina was content to sit quietly and absorb the wonder of the morning. There were no doubts in her mind, no questions to be faced, and no decisions to be wrestled with.

Watching Rogan slice the water like Poseidon in the Aegean Sea was enough. Rogan was right: Now she'd done it. But in spite of his frantic pace, which clearly spoke of his misgivings, she knew that he'd felt something special too.

Carolina could understand his confusion. He'd alienated himself from the world, and she'd intruded. She understood alienation; she'd had many lonely moments of pain and separation herself. The reasons had been different—he'd chosen and she hadn't— but the end result was the same. Still, he was wrong about one thing: *It* would happen again.

And then he turned and was swimming back to the boat. He pulled himself to the dock and stood in the sunlight, totally nude, allowing the water to drip from his body.

"Good morning, Captain."

Rogan, who was slinging the water from his hair, looked up and stopped. She was wrapped in white, her lovely head and face silhouetted like an angel's against the sun. She leaned forward, smiling, and he felt all the regrets he'd wrestled with for the last hour melt away.

"Good morning, Carolina."

"My, how formal. What happened to 'my darling Carrie,' or even 'Goldilocks'?" she teased, but the question in her voice gave away her uncertainty.

Rogan let out a silent groan. Above him, Carolina held out her hand and smiled, as if it were the most natural thing in the world, as if she had some inner serenity that his gruffness didn't touch.

She gave him another tentative smile, stood, and spun away, clasping her sheet like a sarong. "Are you feeling strong enough to give my cooking a second try? If not, we could eat peaches."

"I'm not hungry," he said, and began to climb again. "I have to go into town and consult a practicing attorney. I'll just get something there."

"May I come too?"

"No!" he snapped, and knew he was overreacting. Her puzzled expression was erased from her face, leaving a protective mask in its place.

"Rogan, I don't want to make you uncomfortable. But ever since that first night you brought me here, I've known this had to be, that we had to be. Why do you insist on fighting it?"

"Carolina, I didn't bring you here. I don't know why you keep talking like that."

"I'm afraid I don't have any experience in how I'm supposed to act the morning after, but somehow I thought it was the woman who had second thoughts, not the man."

Rogan walked up the ramp and reached for a towel that was hanging on the rail. With little bashfulness, he dried himself thoroughly before wrapping the towel around his lean hips in such deliberate motions that she realized he was delaying his response.

"Carolina, I apologize for what happened. I was angry that anybody had made you feel inferior, that your own father had suggested that you were less than a woman. What I did was simply to show you that you are desirable, that any man would be proud to have you."

She flinched. "Any man but you?"

"It isn't that. I just don't make commitments anymore." But he had, he thought as quickly as he'd said it. He'd promised to take care of her.

Carolina's tongue rimmed dry lips. Her heart was hammering so loudly that she knew Rogan must surely hear it. "But you have," she whispered, recalling a different promise. "You promised to teach me to cook, and in return I would paint the *Scarlet Butterfly*."

He felt a deep pain in his chest, a hurt that rose up and almost choked him. With every stride he'd made in the water, he'd told himself that what he'd done was wrong. Carolina was vulnerable. She'd expect more than he could give. She'd expect magic, and all he had to give was the illusion. One night of awakening in his arms wouldn't last a lifetime, and he'd been wrong to promise her more.

Still, as he glared at her, and saw her lips quivering and her proud chin jutting out in defiance, he felt his resolve crumble.

"Besides, Rogan," she went on, "you told my father that you'd take care of me. I don't think I could be so wrong about what happened between us last night. It was special to you too. I'm not asking for forever—just this, for now."

As moisture gathered in her eyes, he gathered her in his arms, burying her face against his chest. The trembling left her body as she leaned against him. And Rogan knew that he'd never had a choice.

"Please, make love to me again, my knight in shining armor. We don't know," she added impishly, "there may be demons in the woods who will try to take my Sir Galahad prisoner, and I may never see him again."

There were demons, all right, but they weren't in the woods—they were in Rogan's mind. There was no fighting them; the temptation being offered was too strong. Involuntarily he slid one arm around her back and the other beneath her thighs and laid her on the deck. "Why are you doing this? How can you be sure?"

"I'm very sure. I want you to make love to your lady, here on deck in the sunlight, so that she can remember you in the long years of your imprisonment."

"This isn't 'Once upon a time,' Carolina, some fairy tale in a book."

"For me it is, Rogan. Don't spoil the fantasy."

He released his towel and flung it away, leaving nothing to hide his desire. And then he kissed her, hard, with urgency, his hand holding her nakedness to the rough thrust of his body.

This time he wasn't gentle, but this time she didn't want gentleness. She accepted and welcomed his desire as he branded her body with playful nips, reveling in the knowledge that she could bring this taciturn man to such a loss of control. When she was finally writhing in agony, he lifted himself and plunged inside.

She vaguely understood that he was responding with his emotion, allowing his need to carry him past reason, past control. He was loving her, but he would not give in to the admission. She understood. And if she could make him see how right they were together, his fear would change with time. She had found her way out of despair, and so would he.

But in a moment all thoughts were erased, as she was caught up in the force of passion, swept into a release of such intensity that she was left sated and limp before she came back to reality.

"Damn!" Rogan came to his knees and swore again, not angrily, but in resignation. He marched across the deck and went below. She could hear him grumbling, and Bully's echoing response. There was another noise that filtered through, a different kind of curse—a thump at the far end of the boat that might have been the ship hitting the dock, or a fist planted against the mast.

Carolina lay on the deck, in the sun, and let its heat sink into every pore. Rogan was slamming around below with such violence that she wondered if the cabin would survive his getting dressed. She smiled. If he weren't emotionally involved in their budding relationship, she thought, he wouldn't re-act so violently. So each curse, each bump, widened her smile.

Then she heard him returning. Risking his wrath, she opened her eyes and took in the sight of him. He'd left his hair free. It was making dark wet spots on the blue chambray shirt he was wearing. From where she was lying on the deck, her gaze could move leisurely up long legs encased in worn jeans.

His rough, strong face was lined with discord as he spoke. "Carolina, this is wrong. I know it, but I don't seem to be able to resist you."

"You haven't done anything that I haven't welcomed."

There was a guttural sound of despair as Rogan shook his head. "I'll be back this afternoon. Don't stay out here too long or you'll blister."

And then he was gone.

But long afterward she was still experiencing the incredible satisfaction he'd given her. She didn't know yet where she was going. She only knew that she'd begun a journey and she couldn't turn back. She wondered what he was feeling now.

What Rogan was feeling as he sat at a table in Ida's house was anger, masked by a brooding silence.

"So where's Beauty this morning?" Ida finally prompted as she poured Rogan a second cup of coffee.

"On the *Butterfly*."

"How is she feeling?"

"Frisky!"

"Uh-huh. And how are you?"

"Hell, I don't know. Where's Harry?"

"Fishing, probably. Why?"

"Where'd he get peaches?"

"Harry brought you peaches? I don't think so. When he left here he had fried pies from Miss Lucy and a couple of fish, but no peaches."

"There were peaches in the galley. Fresh sweet yellow peaches."

"Beats me. Sounds like one of the local variety. There used to be some late producers around, but I thought they were all gone."

So Harry hadn't brought them. He'd hoped Ida

would say she'd sent them, but she hadn't. Bully's phrase, "Peaches for Carrie," kept swirling around in his head. Rogan stood and stalked to the window, glaring out at the river, now calm in the sunlight.

"Rogan, what's really on your mind? I can't see you getting excited about peaches. What's wrong?"

"Wrong? I have a woman, a mythical creature on my boat. It's as if she has some kind of magical powers. Every time I come near her I turn into Samson—a bald, powerless Samson."

"I've heard that happens to men when they fall in love," Ida said quietly.

"I am not in love. I will never fall in love, and furthermore, I don't believe in fate or ghosts or shadow figures! Do you understand that?"

He swore and whirled around to reinforce his point. Ida looked stunned at Rogan's outburst. He grimaced, let out a deep breath of apprehension, and shook his head.

"Sorry, Ida. I have no right to bark at you because I've run into a situation I can't get a handle on. It's just that Carolina doesn't see me as I really am. She's trusting and beautiful and much too gentle for a renegade like me."

"Yep, Beauty and the Beast. Believe me, I've met the Beast. I'll admit that you two put a different twist on the story: Beauty wants to stay and the Beast is trying to get rid of her. Ah, well, you'll work it out, Rogan. In the meantime, try not to growl. You'll frighten her."

"Her?" *Frighten Carolina?* No, it was Rogan who was scared silly, and he knew it.

He still had a half hour before it was time for his appointment with the attorney he was to consult about his court fight over the *Scarlet Butterfly*. On impulse, he stopped at the local bookstore and bought a copy of *Cooking Made Easy*. Carrie ought to be able to follow these recipes, he thought, then went back and exchanged it for a gourmet cookbook. No point in making it too easy on her. On the way to the checkout counter he picked up a copy of a new novel rich with history of Georgia's sea islands and its people. Carrie would like that too.

Carrie. There was something nice about shortening her name, something intimate, he decided as he flung his parcel through the open window of the truck. He climbed in, slammed the door, and leaned his head against the steering wheel. What was he doing, buying paints and books? He was just prolonging the inevitable—her leaving.

The attorney told Rogan about what he'd expected, that the laws were absolute. Any waterway that had ever been navigated by raft, dugout, or boat was state property to which the salvage law applied. Any historical object found in state waters belonged to the state. Even with proof of ownership, Rogan's claim to the *Butterfly* was questionable. Without proof, the state had every right to claim it and would undoubtedly win any court case. And he had less than ten days before he'd meet the state representatives and learn the schooner's fate.

Rogan was hungry and out of sorts as he drove back to the *Butterfly*. He hadn't expected any resolutions. He'd read up on the law and knew he was fighting a losing battle. Even if there were references to the ship and Captain Rogan in Carolina's journal, the journal was gone.

• • •

Carolina never intended to fall asleep on deck, but the sun was warm and she felt so tired—good, but tired. Still, this chronic tiredness seemed to fall away a little more each time Rogan touched her. She closed her eyes and lay there, enjoying the afterglow.

When she finally woke, it was with a start, as if she'd been nudged. Struggling, she tried to open her eyes, feeling a definite shake of her shoulder.

She was alone and in such pain that she couldn't believe it. Her skin was on fire. Every inch of her was bright pink. The midday sun had kissed her delicate skin and left it red and throbbing.

Forcing herself to her feet, she took one agonizing step after another until she reached the shower. With an audible prayer she pulled the string, hoping that the cistern was still filled with rainwater. It was.

The warm water sluiced across her body, but gave only temporary relief to the heat that was increasing with every moment. At least she was clean. Rogan had called her a puny, bony little thing. Now she was cooked too. "Ohhhh!" she groaned as she made her way to the cabin and fell backward on the bed.

"Ohhhh!" she repeated, trying desperately to marshal some of the strength she'd garnered from her captain. Yes, she was in pain, but it wasn't the excruciating kind of pain she'd once felt inside her head. This was intense, but it would pass. She could concentrate. She would lie there and not move.

Taking shallow, quick breaths, she finally slept again. By late afternoon she roused briefly, feeling the cooling touch of liquid being applied to her skin.

There was an allusive scent to the lotion and a gentleness to the application.

"Rogan?" she whispered, and started to open her eyes. But they wouldn't open. They were swollen shut.

"Be still, Carrie. I'll take care of you."

There was something stiff about his voice, something different, but she didn't know what. She only knew that Rogan was there, and that he was soothing her with his touch and his words, just as he had the first night when she'd collapsed in his arms.

"I know, Rogan. You always do."

She felt his fingers falter a moment as they grazed her breast and moved lower. Even in her state of pain she felt a response, a shiver of anticipation for what she expected to come. But he simply ranged across her abdomen and down her thighs, applying the liquid until he'd covered everything but her face.

His fingertips spread coolness across her face, her swollen eyelids, her cheeks, lingering on her lips. *"Your hair,"* he whispered in a gravelly voice, *"your lovely hair. Let it grow again—for me."*

"Of course, Rogan. I'll do anything you ask."

When Rogan stepped on board there was no sign of Carolina. He called her name, first lightly, then with a thundering voice that set Bully to squawking wildly.

"Hoist anchor, furl the mast! Looky, looky, looky—"

"Shut your beak, you loudmouth, or I'll pull your claws out one at a time. Where's Carrie?"

"Carrie!"

Rogan heard the thundering voice calling her name.

It had to be his own, but he couldn't remember saying it.

"Rogan?"

She was in the cabin. He took the steps in one leap, reaching the bed and coming to a stunned stop. She was one pitiful sight. She was blistered so badly that her eyes were closed. Her face was swollen, and her arms were extended out so that they wouldn't touch her body.

"Great heavens! You're cooked!"

"Well, you wanted me to learn how," she managed weakly.

"But I didn't intend for you to start with yourself. Does it hurt?"

"Not as much since you put that lotion all over me."

She was hallucinating. There was an odd-looking bottle of liquid on the table by the bed, a bottle without a label. She must have found it in his chest and used it before she got so feverish. No point in upsetting her by denying her claim. Instead he knelt beside her. "Would you like more lotion?"

"Oh, yes. I like you touching me."

He quickly remembered that he liked touching her too—too much, so that what started out as a medicinal effort soon became an intense test of willpower. Carolina was in no condition to move, and yet her nipples puckered in response beneath his touch. On the way back home, when he ought to have been trying to find a way to keep his ship, he'd been searching for a way to let Carolina go, starting with a vow that he wouldn't touch her again. He'd allow her to stay on board until they could find a solution to her future, but nothing more.

He was a strong man. He could control his emotions. He was old enough to refuse to give into base sexual urges and to explain to Carolina why it was better that they refrain from lovemaking. There were hundreds of men out there better suited to her. She owed it to herself to look over the market and make sure she wasn't mistaking a simple crush, or lust, or even gratitude, for more.

But it wasn't working. His heart was pounding; he was hard and throbbing. With effort, he pulled air into lungs that felt as if they were as blistered as the skin he was touching.

"Oh, Rogan, I wish I could open my eyes and see you."

"Why?"

She licked her parched lips. "You're so beautiful, so gentle, so special. Thank you for caring—"

She would have finished, but his lips brushed hers once, then again. "Your lips were cool before, Rogan. They're warm now."

Before? "Just lie here and rest. I'll fix you something cool to drink."

"Yes, I'd like that. I'd like crushed ice and peaches, like you brought earlier."

Rogan started to argue, then he saw the glass with tiny slivers of peach swimming in the melting liquid. This was very strange. Carolina was probably describing what she'd imagined, what she herself had done, what she'd fantasized.

But what about the glass?

And what about the peaches?

Seven

Carolina dreamed again, but she dreamed almost every time she slept now, hazy impressions of Rogan. Sometimes he was dressed in his shorts. Sometimes he took on the persona of Captain Jacob. Jacob was always tantalizingly close, yet just out of her vision.

This dream was different. Whisper-soft hands applied lotion to her hot body, followed later by cream-covered, rough fingers that both tingled and soothed. She squirmed and moaned, and not altogether from the pain of the sunburn.

Rogan wanted to slip back in bed with her, but the dragons that warred inside his mind were too strong. He should have taken her to town before he'd let his sense of responsibility take over. Hell, when would that have been? He'd felt responsible the moment he laid eyes on her, as if they'd bonded immediately in some old-world, mystical alliance.

Rogan sighed and covered his charge with a sheet.

He was shocked at her flushed pink skin. The September sun would not have blistered a normal skin, but Carolina's, protected so long from the elements, was tender. He didn't think she'd be ill, for the lotion was already making a difference. But he was stunned by his ever-growing protective instincts.

He replaced the cork in the bottle and studied it again. The container was old, but the lotion inside was fresh. There was a citrus scent to the liquid and a creamy texture that he didn't recognize. When he'd moved from his condo in Savannah to St. Marys he'd spent several days at Ridgeway Inn, storing some of his things in Ida's root cellar. Perhaps when he'd left he'd inadvertently picked up someone else's medication without being aware of it.

Carolina was sleeping quietly now, the rise and fall of the sheet evidence of that. He fed Bully and made himself a sandwich, of which he took two bites before discarding it. For the first time, the *Scarlet Butterfly* withheld its peace. Granted, his talk with the lawyer had been unsettling, but he'd expected that. He'd expected Carolina to be there when he returned too. But finding her sleeping in his bed again, flushed and feverish, had unnerved him.

Moonlight dappled the deck with lacy patches of light, the tree limbs throwing shadows between them. Rogan lay thinking about the other Carolina and Rogan, the hammock swaying gently as the ship undulated in the water. It was just as he was sliding into sleep that he noticed the vague shadow near the galley, a dark silhouette of a man wearing a captain's hat. Imagination, he scoffed mentally. For a moment he actually thought someone was standing there.

"Carolina?"

There was no answer and the shape seemed to absorb into itself and disappear. But the faint smell of tobacco that always lingered around the ship was stronger. This time Rogan decided to check it out.

Quietly he slipped off the ship and down the gangplank to shore. In the shadows, he stopped and waited. But there were no sounds to indicate an intruder, and the tobacco smell was too faint to follow. As always, it seemed to center on the *Butterfly*. Rogan had never worried about himself, but Carolina was under his protection now. Nothing, he vowed, was going to happen to her.

He'd bought a cookbook to satisfy that part of their arrangement, and the ship's restoration was almost finished. As soon as the portrait of the schooner was done, he'd find a place for Carolina in town, perhaps at the inn. That way, if they decided to do so, they could continue to see each other.

Ida could take care of her.

Carolina needed taking care of.

Sean flexed his fingers. The tips still tingled with coolness, a residual effect of the lotion he'd rubbed on Carolina's body.

Carolina.

It was all he could do to stop himself from going below to check on her again.

As Rogan slept, the ship rocked on the water. Carolina dreamed.

And the curious shadow that was neither man nor spirit glided forth along the deck, like a sentry on watch. Thoughts leaped out of the void and voiced themselves in his mind as he paced the old, familiar deck.

Heaven above, how can I be here? Why am I here? Carolina is falling in love with this man. And I can't stop her.

Jacob felt a great sense of urgency. He didn't know why, but he knew that he didn't have much time.

The next morning Carolina could hardly walk. Though she was still sore, the sunburn had already begun to fade. But clothes? She couldn't abide the thought. Instead, she slid into another of Rogan's T-shirts, a dark green one that came to mid-thigh. Climbing the stairs, she felt a slight tingle in her hand, the kind of sensation that once signaled the approach of a dreaded seizure. But it soon stopped and she forgot about it as she heard the sound of hammering.

With a vengeance, Rogan was nailing planks in the hole on deck. He didn't know she was watching, though she noticed his glancing across at the opposite shore and back. There was something primitive about this man, something elemental that stirred her as deeply as the woman for whom she'd been named must have responded to Jacob.

Suddenly Rogan stood and whirled around. He caught sight of her and snapped, "Don't sneak up on me like that!"

"I'm sorry. You were making so much noise that I didn't think you'd hear me."

Then he looked concerned. "I'm sorry, did I wake you? I'm so used to being the only one here that I didn't think. At least I was until last night; now I'm not sure."

"You mean there's someone else here?"

"No, . . . well, maybe. I mean I can't see him, but I feel him. He's watching me, the bas—" He cut himself off, caught by the sight of her—hair disheveled, looking like a child who'd just come from her bath, all scrubbed and pink. "How is your sunburn?"

"It's much better, thanks to your help. You must have used the entire bottle of medicine."

His head jerked up in surprise. There'd been half the bottle left when he'd gone to bed. "But I didn't—" He stopped. If there were some kinky bastard slinking around applying lotion to sleeping women, he didn't need to alarm Carolina. Instead he inspected her, examining her with as medical an expression as he could muster, considering that all he could see was the lovely body his shirt was hugging.

She didn't flinch. The woman was entirely too trusting. He let out a long breath. "Well, it does seem to have worked. You aren't nearly so red as I expected you to be. Maybe I'll put on more lotion. Bring the bottle to the galley."

"But it wasn't on the table by my bed when I woke. Didn't you do something with it?"

"No, I left it there."

They stared at each other for a puzzled moment. "Well, it's probably on the floor somewhere. After I make breakfast I'll look." She turned toward the galley.

"Ah, Carolina, I bought you a cookbook," Rogan called out. "It's on the table."

"Thanks." Carolina tried to appreciate his thoughtfulness, but all she could think about was the fact that one condition of her staying was that she learn to cook. He was trying to hasten that. She leafed through the pages of the book, read the complicated gourmet recipes, and smiled. She might learn to cook, but not from this book, and not right away. Rogan was putting out a mixed message. She wondered if he was fooling himself, and decided that it didn't matter.

Carolina hummed softly as she peeled the peaches on the counter, then located a box of flake cereal and bowls. She tried to copy Rogan's making of the coffee. Once it finished perking, she sampled the hot liquid and decided that it was a little strong, but close enough.

"Rogan, come and eat."

At a water barrel outside the galley, Rogan washed his face and hands, slinging the water across the deck as the sun dried his skin. He'd thought about Carolina all the time he was working, chastising himself for making love to her. Even if her overbearing father had convinced her that she was unappealing, Rogan had no right to touch her. Loving her tied her to him more closely, and he knew about women and their nesting instincts.

He'd just about persuaded himself to treat her as a boarder, an employee, a deckhand, when he stepped into the galley and caught sight of her leaning down to take the milk from the refrigerator. Deckhands didn't borrow his T-shirts, and they certainly didn't show their bare bottoms to the boss.

"Goldilocks," he said in a voice that was much too gravelly. "I think we'd better invest in some fashionable long dresses for you."

"Long dresses?" She closed the refrigerator door and turned, placing the milk on the table.

"Yes, with high necklines and long sleeves."

"Why, Captain." She smiled and took two steps that brought her to him. "Why would you want to do that?" She couldn't let that strained expression remain on his face. The day was too beautiful. He was too beautiful. She put her arms around his neck and reached up to kiss him.

Sean turned his head so that all she found was his cheek. "So I won't—you won't—get sunburned." He unclasped her hands and slid past her. Taking his seat on the bench, he turned enthusiastically to the food.

"More peaches?"

"Yes, they were here on the counter. I thought you must have seen Harry again this morning."

"Nobody has been here except the two of us. Though last night I did think I might have seen— Never mind. I'm going to have another look along the shore. If somebody is spying on us, he's probably just curious about a woman on board."

"Shore?" Her face became even more flushed. "Do you think he was watching yesterday when we— when I was sleeping on deck after we—after you left?"

"You fell asleep? That makes more sense. I was afraid you were one of those foolish women trying to get a tan, until I realized you were blistered on only one side."

"I haven't thanked you for putting me to bed and taking care of me. That's becoming a habit."

Sean frowned at Carolina. "That's the second time you've said something about me helping you. I didn't."

"Of course you did. That first day I was walking down the road and I grew very dizzy. Suddenly there you were, in your captain's clothes and cap. You carried me back to the *Butterfly* and put me to bed."

"Carolina, the first time I laid eyes on you was when I walked into my cabin and found you under my sheet."

"But that can't be. You comforted me and told me you'd take care of me. I felt you. I heard you."

"You were just weak and confused."

Carolina stood, eyes wide, her breath coming fast and shallow. "Sean Rogan, I've been weak and confused for a long time. But not about you, not about being here. I know that I passed out, but I saw you. I felt the rough texture of your coat against my cheek. I smelled your pipe tobacco, so you can quit sneaking around smoking."

"Rough texture of my coat, in all this heat?"

"Yes, I did—at least I thought I did."

"And did you see me lift you from the deck and put you to bed yesterday too?"

"Yes . . . well, no. I think I walked. Then later my eyes were closed. I mean my lids were swollen, and I couldn't open them. But I felt you and smelled you and heard your voice. It was you, Rogan. And you can stop playing games with me!"

He started to say that she'd been dreaming, but it wouldn't have satisfied her; that he didn't smoke, but he'd smelled the tobacco too. Whatever the answer was, she really believed that he'd brought her on board and cared for her. And for a moment, Rogan wished it were so.

Still, she did get on board, which left two possibilities. Either Carolina was the one who was playing games, or there was someone else on board. There were too many unexplained happenings: the tobacco, the lotion, even the peaches that appeared mysteriously.

"Perhaps you're right, Carolina. I'll search again."

Rogan left the galley and made his way down the ramp to the dock and into the trees, where he forced himself to stop and listen. There were no sounds indicating that either the woodland creatures or the marsh animals were being disturbed. After letting out a deep breath, he began to look around.

Only his footprints and Carolina's were visible, but that was to be expected. Undaunted, he crept into the brush, moving quietly, studying, examining, determined to find physical evidence of the presence he'd sensed for several days.

On board the *Butterfly,* Carolina put away the breakfast things. The sun was trying to climb above the tree line, but it seemed caught in the limbs of the pines so that piercing arrows of gold penetrated their foliage.

Carolina gathered up the painting supplies that Rogan had bought for her and made her way on deck. She found a spot overlooking the lake where she could see the river. She sat in the shadows, with her canvas in the sunlight. First she'd select and paint the site, then she'd move onto the bank and sketch in the ship.

Now and then she heard Rogan—or at least she hoped it was Rogan—moving around the small lake. At one point she watched him swim across the river and pull himself from the water on the other side.

But she soon lost herself in her drawing. And to her surprise she found she didn't need to move to shore to see the lines of the *Butterfly*. The sketch was rough, but it was good. A feeling of confidence surged through her as she tried to capture all her feelings for the ship. At first just a phantom, it soon took shape and form.

Finally she leaned back and studied her effort. The *Scarlet Butterfly*'s canvases were unfurled, caught by the wind as it skimmed along the water. Its graceful bow lifted in flight.

"There's something wrong."

Rogan was back. She studied her drawing. What's wrong?

"It's the figurehead, lass. The carving of the Scarlet Butterfly *is missing from her bow."*

She hadn't heard him come on board, but her senses recognized him, and his deep voice confirmed it. He wasn't angry anymore. And he was right. There should have been a figurehead. She turned, her face filled with joy. But no one was there.

For a long moment she waited, feeling his presence, yet not seeing. And as she watched, she began to see. Little by little a shadow materialized, becoming more solid, more real, more recognizable. The blue coat. The captain's cap. The pipe. Was her mind playing tricks on her? No. She knew this man. She'd felt him, visualized him, and dreamed about him. Now she understood. He was smiling at her, but his lips were drawn with sadness, his eyes confused and filled with pain.

"You're Jacob Rogan, aren't you?" she whispered.

"You can see me?"

"Yes, I can see you. I think I've seen you all along."

"I suspicioned so. And you're Carrie, but you're not."

"No, I'm Carrie's descendent. Are you real?"

"I'm not certain. Suddenly I was here and you were swooning in my arms. Since then I cannot seem to go back to wherever I was—or perhaps I've been here all along."

"You can talk to me?"

"So it seems."

"But not to Rogan."

"No, I think not—at least, not yet."

Carolina closed her eyes. She'd been warned that radiation could damage the body, that the resulting memories, and even behavior, could be distorted. But nobody had warned her about this kind of thing. It was so real; Jacob seemed as real as Rogan.

Rogan! Surely he could see Jacob. Then he'd know that she wasn't dreaming or imagining things. "Rogan!" she called out, rushing to the side of the boat where she'd last seen him. "Rogan!" she called more urgently, "Come back, please!"

"Carolina?" Rogan's anxious voice answered from the woods across the lake. "Are you all right?"

"Yes! Hurry!"

Moments later Rogan was climbing over the side and striding to meet Carolina. "What's wrong?"

"Oh, Rogan, you were right. There was someone here, but not what you thought. Come, you must see for yourself." She tugged him back to the spot where she'd set up her painting, a frantic expression on her face. "Look!"

But there was no one there.

"He's gone. He was here, Rogan."

Rogan looked around. He saw nobody; nor could anyone have escaped without Sean having seen him, for he'd had his eye on the ship from the moment Carolina had called out.

"Who, Carolina? Who did you think you saw?"

"I saw—" Then she stopped. If he'd thought she was hallucinating before, he'd likely think she'd gone over the edge if she told him now that she'd seen a ghost. "I was sketching when I saw him. As clear as day, I saw him on the deck of this schooner. He told me about the missing figurehead." She could see the skepticism dawning in Rogan's eyes. "I did, Rogan—at least I thought I did."

"'He' who?"

"Well, don't laugh, but do you think that what we've been seeing might be a ghost? Do you think it's possible that Jacob stayed here on his ship?"

"Of course not. There are no such things as ghosts." Rogan's voice held far more certainty than he felt.

He turned his attention to Carolina's canvas, and was stunned. When he'd asked her to paint a portrait of the *Butterfly,* he had intended it as therapy. It had never occurred to him that she had such talent.

"The figurehead," he said quietly. "How did you know? I mean I haven't found it yet. But I knew there was one."

"That's what I was trying to tell you," she said. "It was as if a voice came to me, describing the carving of a scarlet butterfly on the figurehead. Oh, Rogan, do you suppose it's still in the water?"

"I don't know. If it's in the mud, we may never find it. If it wasn't made from cypress it might not have survived. Wood worms or warm water could have destroyed it; the tide could have washed it out to sea. I don't know."

"But we could look, couldn't we?"

"Carolina, we don't even know that there *was* a butterfly, and we don't know whether the figurehead was saved or left to decay. It could take a lifetime."

Clasping Rogan's arms with both of her small hands, Carolina spoke with authority. "Sean Rogan, even if you don't believe in ghosts, I know that figurehead is in this lake, and we're going to find it."

"Look at the water, Carolina darling. Do you see the bottom?"

"Of course not. That water is as black as ink."

"And just as hard to see through," Rogan said, trying to quell the flicker of excitement that was already tugging at his equilibrium. He had enough to do. He wasn't about to involve Carolina in a futile search for an object they might never find, even if she did actually believe the captain's ghost had told her about the carving.

Of course there was no ghost. But there was no sign of any human anywhere he'd searched either. He'd lived on the *Butterfly* for almost nine months and he'd seen no sign of a spirit. Of course the ship groaned and creaked; that was to be expected. And now and then he'd had the feeling that somebody was watching him, but that, he told himself, had come from loneliness.

Ghosts didn't take on human form. Ghosts couldn't lift a woman and carry her. Ghosts didn't smoke pipes or wear rough jackets. They didn't gather peaches and leave them as gifts.

But at the moment he lacked a better explanation, and Sean Rogan didn't like anything he couldn't explain or control.

Now, with Carolina's blue eyes sparkling with excitement and her lovely face peering up at him, he forgot his earlier resolve not to touch her. He ached to touch her, to tell her that once he'd believed in dreams. And he ached for himself, because he knew how hard dreams die, and how all his plans to stay away from her until he could figure out a way to get her to Ida's were vanishing.

"It might be a dream, Rogan, but can't we try and make it real?"

There was no smile on Rogan's face as he gazed down with a solemn expression. She wished he didn't look so lost. She wished that he hadn't been hurt so badly that he couldn't join in a simple let's-pretend kind of wish. He seemed so sure of himself, she thought, yet there were times, like now, when the vulnerability showed through.

Carolina stood on her toes, stretching to reach him. Her breasts skimmed his chest, throbbing beneath the T-shirt as she breathed. "I think that my coming here, fulfilling my dream, was somehow meant to be. Once I thought my life was over, but I lived. I think that you came out here not to be alone but because you'd lost your dreams. We were both looking for something. I wasn't certain what it was until today, when suddenly I felt the comfort and peace the *Butterfly* offered. Oh, Rogan, it's a sanctuary."

Rogan released the breath he'd been holding. The sun leapt over the pines and its rays fell full across them, catching the gold in Carolina's hair and showering her with ethereal light. He leaned closer, unable to stop himself any longer from touching the lips that begged for his kiss. And he said with his lips what he couldn't say in words—that she was right about dreams; that he'd left them all behind, until he'd found the *Butterfly* and her.

When Beth had died, he'd used his family's squabbles as an excuse to turn away. He'd become a dried-out, emotionless man who'd lost tomorrow. Carolina was so bright and so confident. As his hand moved along the small of her back, it started again, that incredible need, a need for the kind of solace that he had no right to desire.

"Ah, Carrie," he whispered, and shook his head. His lips curled into a tight smile but his eyes filled with regret. "I wish it were that easy, darling, but it isn't. I think your imagination is promising you something false. Don't plan on me, or this, or a future here. I should have taken you back. Keeping you here is selfish; it's for me, and I know that. When you're better, we'll have to talk."

Carolina felt an icy spear cut through her. She let her arms fall away from his neck. He was wrong. He didn't understand. But he would—sooner or later. Meanwhile, she'd give him time to learn.

"Aye, aye, Captain. I'll stop kissing you, if you insist. But I'm not going to stop thinking about it. I'll just have to find something else to occupy my time. Right now, I'm going to work on my painting, while the feeling is still here. Maybe the captain will give me a hint about the figurehead."

"Fine," Rogan snapped, then forced himself to soften his words. "I have sanding to do and the new wood to seal and varnish."

"First, food. You didn't eat breakfast. I think I can manage a salad without a cookbook, if that's all right."

"Fine. I'll make iced tea."

This time they worked together, touching subtly and not so subtly. Carolina stole two quick kisses, giving promises of things to come with her eyes. After they'd eaten and cleared away the food, Carolina went back to her picture and Rogan to the sanding and polishing of the wood he'd used to repair the hole. He'd thought at the time that the hole had been chopped clumsily in the deck, but he'd pushed the thought aside. Now as he worked he allowed his mind to consider the possibility that Captain Jacob had deliberately scuttled his ship here, in a pond near where he'd later built his home.

Why? Carolina's journal seemed to suggest flight, fear on her part. And Jacob? Had he been a willing participant, or some kind of pawn? As he worked Sean found himself glancing at Carolina. He liked her serious expression, her shapely legs folded Indian style beneath her as she leaned forward intently, then back as she considered her strokes.

The afternoon set the pattern for the next few days. With Bully's cage outside on deck, Sean would work on repairing the ship and she'd paint. And they learned that there was more to their being together than making love.

Occasionally she gave him a quick side glance and a smile, as if she knew a secret and planned to tease him until she was ready to reveal it. They talked about books and movies. She found that Rogan was a Groucho Marx fan. She confided that, because the doctors thought laughter promoted healing, she'd spent hours watching the Three Stooges while she'd been housebound.

And little by little, Rogan began to laugh. She

exchanged her soft T-shirt for a bathing suit, and her skin began taking on the color of warm honey.

One afternoon she voiced the question she'd deliberately withheld. "Rogan, tell me about your family."

"You don't want to hear that. It might spoil your creativity."

"I want to know everything about you. And I want you to know about me."

"That isn't a good idea." But he found he wanted to know about this woman who was changing before his eyes. With a brush in her hand, she seemed to gather life from the river and the *Butterfly*. Her eyes were softer, bluer, and she seemed more content.

"All right, but you first, Carrie."

This time when the deck creaked, Rogan was expecting it. He'd come to associate that response with the name Carrie.

"My life isn't very exciting. My father, as you already know, is an attorney, very wealthy and very powerful. Part of his money came from his father and the rest he's made representing people who pay him great sums to make their lives easier. He's brilliant, and he's determined."

"Sounds pretty tough. What about your mother?"

"My mother wasn't a well woman. She might have loved my father once, but I only remember her trying desperately to pretend that she was strong when she wasn't. She refused to take care of herself, staying out late at night, drinking too much, smoking too much, and I suspect taking too many prescription drugs. Again and again she'd leave."

"If she was so unhappy, why didn't he let her go?"

"My father doesn't know how to lose anything: a case, a wife, a daughter."

"But he did," Rogan corrected. "He eventually lost your mother, and he's lost you."

"Yes, but I didn't have to die to get away."

That stopped Rogan for a minute. He wondered if she might have come closer to dying than she'd admitted.

"I'm sorry. Your father must be a very lonely man."

Carolina transferred a sketch to her canvas. She gave a look of satisfied approval and turned to the tubes of oils, selecting a brush and squeezing dabs of color onto the palette.

"I never thought much about it, but maybe you're right. He thinks that anything he wants, he'll get, and if there's a problem, he'll find an answer. He was always good to me, but he just wouldn't listen."

"I can understand that. There was a time I was accused of the same thing."

Carolina turned in mock surprise. "You wouldn't listen? I don't believe it."

"Believe it," he said, ignoring her affectionate sarcasm. "I was head of a family business that included two television stations, two newspapers, the largest pecan orchard and candy business in the South, and a chain of resorts in the Caribbean. There was nothing I couldn't do, or arrange, or fix—except the genetic flaws in the family I loved, the family that was killing itself with jealousy."

"I met your brother," Carolina said. "I didn't know he was your brother at the time—he didn't bother to introduce himself. But later Ida told me. Funny, I got the idea that he cared about you. He refused to tell me where you were."

"He knew I'd kill him if he did. Keeping reporters

away from me was part of my . . . retirement agreement."

"But once you started raising the schooner everybody in St. Marys would have known."

"Yes. I thought that I could buy silence. I was wrong."

Carolina laid down her brush and turned to watch Rogan. He'd finished applying the protective coating to his work and was staring out at the river as though he were somewhere else entirely. This time only Rogan filled her sight. Often when she looked at him she'd see Rogan, then somewhere in the background she'd catch a glimpse of another shape, another presence that looked the same yet wasn't.

Jacob. She didn't question it anymore. His presence wasn't threatening. Rather, he brought comfort and a kind of security. She felt as if he were looking after them.

"I see. Other than your brother, the newspaper editor, who else makes up the Rogan family?"

Suddenly he was telling her about the two older sisters who'd decided they wanted a voice in the corporation, and, on being given seats on the board of directors, had taken the advice of husbands and boyfriends, causing such discord that it was all Sean could do to keep the business from disintegrating. He might still have kept things going if his mother hadn't remarried and demanded the right to vote her stock.

"And there is my youngest brother, Ryan. He didn't start out to be a doctor. He thought he was cool. He and my youngest sister were caught up in another life-style, another time. Ryan didn't care about the family, he only cared about—well, it doesn't matter."

It all came back to Rogan. Rescuing Ryan and Beth from one problem after another. The publicity, the lawsuits, the harsh words and hurt that could never be undone. Then Beth had died and Ryan had changed. But by that time it had been too late; the family had been shattered. When the downswing in the economy came along, Rogan couldn't keep the company afloat. His sisters and older brother voted to dissolve the company and sell off its holdings. Ryan didn't care enough to vote. Rogan knew that he was licked.

He could have fought them. He might have won. Instead, Rogan resigned as CEO. The holdings and the cash were divided up, with the sisters receiving a television station and a resort. The pecan orchard and candy business went to his mother and the newspaper to his brother David. Ryan got a house in St. Marys and Rogan took the old family estate on the river.

"Oh, Rogan, I'm so sorry." She cleaned her brush, put away the paint, and came over to sit beside the man who'd been so terribly hurt by those he loved.

"Don't be. I got over it a long time ago."

But he hadn't. She sensed that he was still hurting, just as she was. Love should be healing, but sometimes it brought only pain. Carolina leaned her head on his shoulder and was rewarded by his arm sliding around her, this time in gentle sharing, in acceptance.

For a long time they sat, her presence giving him comfort. Then, Carolina felt Rogan tense, as if he realized what he was doing. He was pulling away.

She came to her feet, scaled the railing at the edge of the ship, and dove smartly into the water.

Rogan watched in amazement as she flipped over on her back and floated like some exotic gold-and-green fish. Then she turned and swam toward shore. As she reached the shallow water, she suddenly froze where she was standing and let out a scream.

In a second he was over the side. When he reached her she had an expression of utter dismay on her face.

"What's wrong, Carrie?"

"Yuck! Mud. I hate it squishing through my toes." She flung herself against him, hanging around his neck, her legs curving around his hips. "I like this much better. Take me to the house, Rogan. You said you would. I want to see where Jacob lived."

"Carolina, you aren't dressed for the woods. There is a trail, but it isn't totally clear."

"You'll take care of me, Rogan. I know you will."

And as he read the trust in her eyes, he knew that he had no choice. He never had.

Eight

"Jacob, I'm too heavy for you to carry. I insist that you let me down."

"For twelve weeks you have insisted this, ordered that, and demanded something else. From now on I shall make the decisions. And I will carry you ashore. One woman, carrying one tiny unborn babe, is child's play after what you've put me through."

Carrie bit back her protest and settled against his massive chest. His arms beneath her back and thighs were firm and strong. It wasn't being carried that was creating such a problem for her, it was the queer shortness of breath and the thundering of her heart that would give her away if she wasn't careful.

For the first two weeks on board the *Butterfly*, she'd alternately cursed and pouted. When she'd enlisted the captain's support she'd expected him to fall at her feet like half the young men in Boston. He hadn't. Over the next two weeks she'd begun to see beyond the captain's stern manner: how he cared for her and for his ship, how he took every precaution that she not be seen. It wasn't until her terrible seasickness, which came with the storm during the fourth week, that his attempt to keep his distance was finally shattered.

Being sick to her stomach was nothing new. She'd felt that way from the first; that was how she'd known she was in the family way. That's why she'd had to run away—to hide her condition from her family so that they wouldn't force her to wed the man they'd chosen for her, the man responsible for her condition, the man who so revolted her that she could give up all she held dear.

Jacob hadn't welcomed her on board his ship. After all, though she was sure he despised the man, he was her father's partner. And all the times he'd come to the house he'd ignored every attempt she'd made to gain his attention. Jacob was a stern, aloof man, much too old for her, but once he'd found her hiding on board his ship, he hadn't been able to refuse her plea for help.

She was already compromised, and he'd be held responsible, no matter the reason. He didn't know about the babe, not at first, for she was concerned about what he might do if he learned the truth. But then came the seasickness, and the retching that came with it.

Carrie had hid the seriousness of her condition for two days. Then, as the third day slid into night and the storm calmed, Jacob had finally forced his way into her quarters and discovered her sad state. He'd undressed her, removed her soiled gown, and pressed little sips of bitter tonic down her to soothe the turmoil. He'd cared for her—wiping the perspiration from her brow, bathing her body in cool water that refreshed. She'd been so sick that she hadn't cared. Then one night she'd finally realized what he was doing.

The roughness of his touch on her skin had given way to a gentleness—and a quiver of excitement—that she'd never expected. Her eyes had opened suddenly, catching a fleeting, yearning expression as his hand rested for a moment on her extended stomach.

"Are you with child, lass?"

She twisted away, ashamed to have him see the answer in her eyes, yet compelled to tell him the truth. *"Yes."*

"And what had you planned to do?"

"I don't know. Find a position in Savannah, perhaps, as a governess or companion. I can sew and care for sick people, and teach children. I am educated," she said proudly.

He'd cast that solemn look at her, a look that said more with its sadness than words could have expressed. *"You know there's a war coming. The South thinks to separate itself from the North. How did you, a mere girl from Boston, expect to find a position in the South?"*

"I hadn't thought. But there must be a parson, or someone, who'd assist me in my search."

"And I suppose you'll tell them you have no husband because he's dead, and you're traveling alone because you have no family member to accompany you?"

She hadn't intended to cry, but by that time she was so worn out and sick that she hadn't been able to hold back the tears. With helpless acceptance he'd taken her into his arms and promised that he'd look after her.

"Oh, Jacob, I feel so horrid. While I was so sick I prayed that I'd lose the child. I was more concerned with myself and the shame. I told myself that I didn't want it. But I was wrong. I do so want my baby. Promise me you'll look after it."

"I will, lass. I'll protect you and the babe. I promise."

And he did. She grew used to the sea, came to revel in the smell of the salt air as the ship slid across the waves. From Savannah he'd sailed south to the islands in the Caribbean, swapping machinery and sugar boxes for spices, fruit, and molasses. Carrie got past her sickness and reveled in the feel of the sea breeze in her hair and the sun on her skin. Jacob even began to laugh now and then. Finally, on the return trip, he made arrangements for her to stay with a woman near the coast while he returned to Boston one last time.

She'd heard rumors of discord for months, though she'd never expected that they'd really have a war. But with the firing of the cannons at Fort Sumter in Charleston Harbor, the war began, and now they were on their way to Lord knew where. Carrie was certain that Jacob would finally be forced to acknowledge the growing attraction that was stealing her breath and turning her insides into vanilla pudding every time he came close to her. But Jacob was a man with an iron will, and she couldn't be certain that her feelings were reciprocated.

"Jacob, are we almost there?"

"Yes, we're here, Carrie."

He left the schooner, carried her through the

water, and was standing on a crudely built porch of a small house beside the lake. He stopped, wanting for the hundredth time to strangle the young woman who'd changed his life, who'd been foolish and brave and had worked her way first into his mind and eventually into his heart.

He'd purposefully sought out this wilderness setting, this marshland with a river to sail and a place to hide his ship. Before leaving Boston he'd been torn between helping the land of his birth and continuing the partnership he had with Carrie's father. He hadn't known which to choose, until he'd learned that the *Butterfly* was destined to carry explosives. Then Carrie had stolen on board his ship and forced him to leave the life he'd always known. He hadn't counted on falling in love with her.

"Captain?"

Rogan felt that prickly sensation again. For a moment he felt as if he were sleepwalking. Then he heard his name called again, pulling him back to the present.

"Rogan! Are you all right?"

Rogan shook off the strange feeling that had swept over him the moment he'd pulled Carolina from the mud and stepped from the water with her in his arms. He moved across the porch and inside the old house. "This is it, Goldilocks, the original Rogan house, built by Captain Rogan—your Jacob, perhaps."

"Oh, yes," Carolina said softly, looking around the room. "Jacob and Carrie. Can't you feel it? They were here, perhaps in this very spot. I wish she'd talked about it in her journal, but she didn't—only about the *Butterfly*. Oh, Rogan, it's wonderful. Can we start restoring it?"

"You aren't going to restore anything. I can't believe you were foolish enough to jump into the water. Suppose there'd been a tree submerged. You could have been hurt."

"Nonsense. I've watched you do the same thing every afternoon when you take your swim. Besides—oh look, Rogan, do you see it?" She caught a glimpse of vivid red, a flutter of wings, hovering in the open window. Then it was gone.

Rogan followed the line of her vision, seeing only a moving leaf from a wild azalea through a crack in the wall.

"What? I don't see anything."

"It was a butterfly—a scarlet butterfly."

"No lass." The voice came to her clearly in the silence. *"The scarlet butterfly has been extinct for a hundred years. It only lived on one small island in the Southern Ocean. Now it's gone."* Carolina looked up at Rogan to see if he'd heard.

Oblivious to the voice, Rogan carried her toward the window and leaned out. "I don't know anything about butterflies, but I don't recall ever seeing a red one."

"Well, I just saw one. Put me down, Captain—eh, Rogan. I want to look around."

"Without shoes, it isn't safe. You could step on a nail, or a snake."

"Nonsense." Carolina kicked her feet and looked up at her knight with a full pout on her lips. "I'll be very careful. I just want to look out the window."

Rogan glanced around. The floor was surprisingly

clean. In fact, he didn't recall it having been so free from debris the last time. He planted Carolina's feet on the floor. She was still dripping wet, his shirt sticking to her slim body like plastic wrap.

"Be careful!" he said sharply in an attempt to push away the odd feeling of unreality that seemed to attack him whenever they were together.

"Oh, Rogan, could it be restored?"

"'Restored'? I doubt it. Rebuilt? Yes. In fact, that's what I'd originally planned to do, until I found the *Butterfly*."

Carolina walked slowly around the rooms and back to the window, as if she were absorbing the aura of the house. She peered out, holding her position for a long time.

"There was a red butterfly here. I know I saw it. The next time we go into town, Rogan, I want a book on butterflies."

More commitment, Rogan thought. Just what he hadn't intended to allow. He couldn't seem to refuse her, even when he knew that what he was doing was wrong.

As she looked out into the trees, Carolina felt a flash of weakness wash over her, a hazy, dizzying uncertainty. She was suddenly tired, so very tired, and she felt disoriented. The trees began to blur, almost disappearing. She held on, refusing to faint. And then she saw it, standing in a clearing—a runty tree, gnarled and bent. And on its limbs were small golden globes of fruit.

"Rogan, I see it."

"The butterfly?" He moved to her side.

"No," she said in a voice filled with awe, "the peach tree. It's here, back there in the woods. I see it."

And then she lost the vision as a gray haze closed out the room and everything in it.

Rogan caught her as she slid to the floor. "Dammit, Carolina! Why do you keep pushing yourself? You're not strong enough to go jumping into the water."

He gathered her into his arms and started back to the ship, feeling her satisfied sigh as she laid her head against his chest.

"I'm fine, Rogan, really I am. It's just that I need—"

"You need rest. You need to stay in bed. I need to send you back to your father. At least he knows how to take care of you."

"No, Rogan, I just need my medication," she whispered under her breath.

He put her back to bed, peeling the wet swimsuit from her body and covering her with a sheet. He was always putting her back to bed, watching her sleep, feeling himself harden at the sight of her. Since she'd arrived he had accomplished little except repairing the hole in the deck. The sails, ordered weeks earlier, were ready—no, waiting—to be picked up.

He needed to start preparing a defense for his claim to the *Butterfly* before the meeting next week. He needed to rebuild the house. He needed to find the figurehead, if in fact there was one. He needed to stop concentrating on the golden-haired woman who'd come into his life with silver-blue eyes and a "hello world" attitude.

He needed to stop smelling imaginary tobacco smoke and hearing creaks and groans that weren't there. He needed to work off some of his frustrations.

Ten minutes later he was walking up the path to the old house. The swim hadn't helped. He went inside and walked over to the window where Carolina had thought she'd seen the butterfly.

"Damn!" He swore and swung at the wall beside the crumbling fireplace. A brick moved and fell to the floor with a thud. The pressure of his blow must have somehow dislodged the brick, even though he hadn't actually touched it. Spooky. Everything about the woman, the storm, the night had unnerved him.

Then, as if he were being directed to do so, he leaned over and studied the hole left by the brick. There was something inside, an oilcloth pouch, tattered now by the passage of time. Inside the pouch was a small book. Carefully, he removed the book and opened it to the cover page.

The private journal of Carolina Walden—May 12, 1860.

Rogan felt a ripple of cold zigzag down his backbone.

More intrusions from the past. First the boat, then the woman. Now an earlier journal.

Rogan was almost afraid to turn the page and find there were no entries. No, he thought. This was Carolina's ancestor too. Besides, he didn't want to leave her alone too long. He'd take the book back to the boat. He gently replaced the book in its pouch and started back to the ship. He was almost at the end of the dock when he heard the voice.

"No. She can't stay. She doesn't belong. You can't protect her."

Sean glanced furtively around. He didn't know whether he'd actually heard someone speak, or whether he'd imagined it. As he stood holding the book he felt a strange tingling in his hands, and smelled the ever-present scent of tobacco.

Back on the ship he held the diary for a time, allowing himself to acknowledge the strange feeling of connection that came with its touch. It had to be Carolina and her strong conviction that they were somehow destined to come together that was feeding his own irrational fantasy. By the glow of the galley light, Rogan carefully removed the book from the pouch and turned to the first page.

Carolina Walden of Boston, Massachusetts. August 12, 1860. We are three days out of Boston and Jacob has not yet spoken to me. I am afraid, but I am determined. I won't go back. And I know that he cares for me, even if he chooses not to show it.

Apparently Carolina kept a full record of her life, at least the life that included Jacob. Sean hadn't been certain that he believed his Carolina's claim to having seen a journal, and he was still unclear about how it came into the Evans's family's possession. He was tempted to wake her and share the diary, but she needed her rest.

My Carolina. He liked the sound of that, then cursed himself for admitting it. She was ingraining herself more deeply with every hour that passed. She was involvement and responsibility—neither of which he needed. There were too many coincidences, too many unanswered questions, and Rogan dealt in absolutes. Maybe it would help, he thought to himself, if he knew about Jacob and his ship.

We made a stop in Charleston to deliver goods and take on more. But word came that a fast new clipper ship out of Boston had docked, and we were forced to leave before Jacob could secure the cargo he sought. All because of me. All because they'll be looking for me, and they'll soon find out that only one ship left Boston Harbor that night.

The reading was slow, the writing fading sometimes to such wavy lines that he couldn't make it out at all. By midnight he'd been able to determine that Carolina had run away from somebody, with Jacob. Poor Jacob. He'd also been a reluctant knight in shining armor. But in the beginning his demeanor had remained cold and distant, leaving Carrie alone and in fear of the man from whom she'd fled.

And they were being followed. Jacob apparently knew so, though he tried, unsuccessfully, to keep it from Carolina.

There were references to the blustery, stern actions of the captain, but no mention was made of the reason for her flight, nor the destination of the *Butterfly*.

Sean leaned back and stretched his neck. He had the uncomfortable impression that he was being watched. Certainly there was nobody around to watch him. He was simply reacting to his conscience over reading someone else's private thoughts. With the prickling sensation still running along his spine, he began to read the diary once more, eager to learn more about the man who'd brought the *Butterfly* there to die.

He doesn't want to leave me, but he must. For days he's paced and stared at the river. I don't think he sleeps, and I try to keep him from knowing that I don't sleep either. The child's coming is still months away, and I feel as if I will break into a thousand pieces if we go on like this.

Yesterday he went into the forest and came back with a tiny wild peach tree that he planted behind the house. He tries to do things to make me more comfortable, but I know he hears the call of the sea. He is at war with his soul. He will go, for he must.

It is late and I write by candlelight. But soon he will come inside. He will make his bed on the floor in the room beyond and we'll each pretend to rest.

No. Not tonight. Tonight I will go to him.

Rogan sat staring at the page, feeling the churning emotions of the writer, the longing of the captain, and the smoldering of the situation they'd been cast into.

He knew, for he was feeling the same things. Night after night he lay in his hammock when all he wanted was to be with her. But she wasn't well, and he didn't think she was emotionally strong enough to handle a turbulent situation that offered no future. The only difference between the past and the present was that his Carolina was not with child. Like Jacob, Rogan had demonstrated willpower he hadn't known he possessed, but so far he'd stayed away.

"What did you do, Jacob? Did you go to her?"

"No. She came to me."

The words were as clear as if someone had spoken them. Rogan looked around, but he was alone in the galley. A fat harvest moon had climbed to a spot above the trees in the west. Long shadows created irregular, pie-shaped wedges of light on the deck, and the rays of the moonlight piped silver along the river's crown of ripples.

Rogan closed the diary and rewrapped it. "Damn! I'm getting squirrelly! I would have sworn that somebody spoke." He returned the journal to the trunk and moved out on deck. He needed some rest before he, too, started seeing butterflies and peach trees and the ghost of Jacob Rogan.

Rogan was worried not only about the changes in his life, but also about Carolina's physical problems. That afternoon's spell wasn't the first time she'd had an attack of weakness. There was a new flush on her face. He'd thought it was a sign of her recovery, but now he wasn't certain. He was worried.

In the cabin below, Carolina was half-awake, half-asleep. After a time she realized that while she was ready for sleep, she was waiting, as she did every night—waiting for Rogan to come to her. There was no doubt that she belonged in his arms, but he couldn't seem to accept that. The schooner, the house, her strange sightings of butterflies and peach trees weren't visions, they were real.

The journal she'd read hadn't mentioned a house. It had only told of a grown woman who'd sailed on her father's schooner, the *Scarlet Butterfly*.

Carolina didn't know what happened to the first Carolina, but she felt a chill of foreboding. Now she was on the same ship, with Rogan, the man she loved, and something was very wrong. For the first time in her life Carolina knew what she wanted, and she was going to lose it.

"Life is precious, Carrie; make the most of what you have. Sometimes we can't fulfill our promises, but we mustn't squander the time we have. You can't wait, lass. You must go to Sean—now. Quickly, before it's too late. Tell him the truth. Tell him that you are in danger."

It was Jacob's voice that came to her; Jacob, who was in tune with her thoughts and needs. Quietly, Carolina climbed the steps to the deck and walked across its polished flooring to the tent of netting. She lifted the fabric and stepped inside.

"Rogan?"

"What's wrong?"

"Jacob says that I'm in danger. You must take me to a doctor." She paused, then implored, "Please hurry!"

Rogan came to his feet, catching his head on the netting and lifting it as he clasped Carolina's arms. Her skin didn't feel right. Neither did her pulse. Something was very wrong.

"You're sick?"

"Not sick exactly. I think that it's just that I haven't been taking my medication."

"Your medication? Hell! I never even thought. Was it in your suitcase?"

"My handbag. I thought I would be all right for a few days. But I guess I need it. Oh, Rogan." She swallowed hard. "I didn't want to be sick. I thought that if I found the *Butterfly*, I'd be strong like *her*."

Rogan gathered Carolina in his arms and strode across the deck.

"The first Carolina was strong, Rogan. She ran away with the captain and left her family and her past behind."

Rogan dressed himself quickly, formulating a plan as he grabbed the sheet from the bed and wrapped Carolina in it.

"Carolina, your great-great-great-great-great-great-great-grandmother ran away with Jacob because she was going to have a child. She didn't want to marry the man her family had chosen, and she coerced Jacob, who was her father's partner, into taking her with him."

"Of course she did," Carolina said happily, allowing Rogan to carry her across to the dock and place her in his truck. "She was in love with the captain too."

Without any idea of how he got off the ship, Rogan suddenly found himself driving like a madman. He'd take her to his brother's clinic, and then he'd call Angus, even if Carolina wouldn't like it.

Rogan groaned. He'd told her father that he'd take care of her. But he hadn't. He'd been so busy trying to keep her from intruding on his life that he hadn't stopped to think what he was doing to hers. Was she in trouble now because of his stubborn refusal to see someone else's needs?

Was his solitude worth it?

Rogan applied more pressure to the gas pedal. Ryan would know what to do. He might not have been able to save Beth, but that didn't mean he wasn't a damned good doctor.

Rogan made a sharp turn and roared down the narrow street that came to a dead end near the ocean. Ryan's house, which contained his small office and free clinic, was one of the original sea captains' houses still standing. There were no lights on. It was after midnight. Saying a brief prayer that his brother was at home and wouldn't refuse him, Rogan lifted Carolina, hurried up the walk, and rang the doorbell urgently.

No answer.

Again he rang, then began to kick the door. "Dammit, Ryan. I know you're in there. Open this door or I'll kick it down!"

The porch light came on and the door opened.

"What's wrong? Sean? Is that you?"

"Of course it's me. Open this door. I have an emergency here, and I need some help."

"You need help? Sean Rogan is asking his brother for help? I don't believe it."

"Believe it, Ryan. There's something wrong with Carolina. Her medicine was lost in the flood, and I didn't know. She's having some kind of reaction."

"Carolina? Bring her in." The man in the hallway swallowed his shock and turned his attention to the problem.

In minutes he had a handle on the situation and was examining the patient, leaving Sean to reach Angus Evans and get the necessary medical information.

Carolina wavered between full awareness and a dreamlike state that greatly concerned Ryan. "It's all right, Doctor," she insisted. "Rogan will take care of me."

"Tell me about the medication, Carolina. What was it?"

"Thyroid and hormones—"

"Why? Why are you taking them?"

Carolina frowned. She couldn't worry about medication. She couldn't seem to remember. All she wanted was to tell the handsome man about the peaches and the scarlet butterfly. But he kept jabbing her with needles, just like they'd done in the hospital.

After several unproductive attempts to find a telephone number for Carolina's father, Rogan remembered the business card in his wallet. He found it and punched in the numbers.

In minutes the man on the other end of the line had arranged to fax Carolina's medical records to

Ryan. Angus Evans held his tongue, neither accusing nor demanding. Rogan would have welcomed his anger. Instead, his silence made the weight of Rogan's error even heavier.

Angus agreed not to fly to Georgia until he received a report from Ryan.

"I should put her in the hospital," Ryan said later after assuring Sean that she was out of immediate danger. "She needs careful monitoring to make certain that her hormones are stabilized. With this kind of problem, endocrine function is crucial. Why on earth didn't she take her medication?"

They were sitting at Ryan's kitchen table, drinking their second pot of coffee. Carolina was sleeping. He would have more lab work done when the commercial facilities opened later in the morning, in order to confirm his findings.

"I didn't know."

"Sean, this woman had a brain tumor. Granted, it was not malignant, but the treatment is radiation. The treatment itself could have severely damaged her pituitary gland, which is responsible for all the body's hormone production. When that happens, those hormones have to be artificially provided."

"I knew about the tumor, I just didn't know she was supposed to be taking medication. And she was afraid if she told me, I'd bring her back to town."

"So?"

"I—I probably would have. No, I'm not sure. The truth is, I didn't want her to go."

"Are you in love with her? No, you don't have to answer that. Nothing less than love would have forced you out of that hole you dug for yourself. I guess I should thank her. I never thought that you would come to me for any reason."

"'Love'? Don't be foolish, Ryan. I'm not in love with Carolina Evans. She's a witch. Ghosts talk to her."

"Well, one of the symptoms of her problem can be mental, but usually once the tumor is gone, the problems disappear. That could mean that the tumor has reappeared."

"The tumor may have reappeared?"

"Only a possibility, brother. Don't panic. More than likely it's the lack of medication, some kind of aberration due to hormone imbalance, or even stress. You of all people ought to understand what stress can do to the mind."

"What do you mean? Dammit it, Ryan, don't you do this to me. I'm not seeing ghosts or long-dead sea captains."

"No, you're too busy isolating yourself from your family."

"Hah! And I suppose the family misses me."

"I doubt that you'll believe me, Sean, but they do. They care about you. They always have."

"And that's why they made my life hell?"

"No, they made your life hell because you closed them out."

"Ryan, you saw what happened once everybody tried to have a say in the operation of the company without considering the consequences. It was chaos."

"They understand that now. They just resented your running roughshod over everybody without allowing for what they might have wanted. Sure, you knew what you doing, and what you were doing was best for them, but, Sean, you were a bastard. I tried to tell you, but as I recall your only comment was a curse and a laugh. I know that I was the only one who understood why you acted that way. But you closed me out too."

Because you were the final hurt, Rogan thought. But he wouldn't talk about Beth, or Ryan's part in her death. She was gone, because of his family. And he'd never forgive them.

"Hell, I thought that it was more than any of you deserved. I was just doing what I had to do to fulfill my obligation."

"Like you did for Carolina?"

Carolina heard their low voices, although they sounded muffled, as if they were on the other side of a thick wall. By being absolutely still and holding her breath, she could make out most of what they were saying. Poor Rogan. He'd been handed the reins of the family business, and then the family had turned into dragons and tried to destroy him. Finally he'd turned his back on them.

Until she'd gotten sick and he'd been forced to ask for help.

She couldn't imagine how she might have felt if Rogan had actually let her father take her away. He hadn't. He'd claimed her, taking responsibility for her, just as he had for his family. He'd given her more than she'd ever expected, and she'd never intended to cause him pain.

What was she going to do?

Rogan watched as Ryan studied the early-morning lab results.

"How is she?" Rogan's voice was tight, his hands deceptively casual as he waited for his brother's answer.

"She's responding to the medication. Now it's simply a matter of monitoring her levels so that she won't have some kind of reaction. She isn't out of the woods yet, but she'd holding her own. It's a good thing you brought her when you did. Why'd you wait so long?"

"I didn't know. I'm not even sure *she* understood the danger. Then last night she came to me and said that Jacob—that I should take her to the doctor. Her voice sounded strange, as if she'd memorized her speech."

"She's still a bit out of it. She keeps smiling and glancing past my head as if she sees someone who isn't there. In spite of her illness, she's really quite beautiful, Sean—certainly not a fruitcake, as David described her."

"She believes that it was fate that brought her here, Ryan, that she's a descendant of the first Carolina Rogan, and she thinks the *Butterfly* is haunted," Rogan said, and came to his feet.

"Haunted? You mean as in a ghost? Have you seen him?"

"No. There is no ghost," Rogan said firmly. "Thank you, Ryan. I'd like to see her, then I have to go." Rogan walked to the bedroom door and glanced inside at the still figure in the white metal hospital bed. In the darkness Carolina made a little sound, drawing him reluctantly to her side.

Rogan watched her sleep. He let out a deep sigh and leaned down to brush her lips with his.

"Get well, Carrie," he whispered. "You wanted to

find the *Scarlet Butterfly*. You thought it was fate, that we belonged together. You were wrong. Jacob sank her himself. I don't know why yet, but I will. I guess you won't understand, but I've already decided that I'll send her back to the bottom before I let them take her. Ryan is right. I'm bullheaded and stubborn. I expect people to do what I think is proper, and maybe I'm learning that what's proper isn't always best."

She wanted to protest, but she couldn't seem to speak. Jacob's there all the time, she wanted to tell him. But Rogan wouldn't have believed her anyway.

"I think Jacob *did* save your life, that it's been Jacob who's watching over you, not me. So you see, love doesn't make things right, Carrie. Both of us ought to know that by now."

Nine

"I'm Ryan, Sean's brother. How are you feeling?"

Carolina opened her eyes.

The man standing in the doorway wearing the white coat over the red Atlanta Braves T-shirt was as impressive as her Rogan, but without the sinister bearing. His hair was short and full, cut in layers just a bit too long, allowing it to hug the collar of his sport shirt. A stethoscope hung around his neck.

"You're the doctor?"

"Yep, the best in St. Marys, Georgia. That's because I'm the only general practitioner here."

"How long have I been here?"

"Three days."

"Where's Rogan?" she whispered.

"Gone back to his schooner to do battle with the state's recovery team on their way to claim the *Butterfly*."

"But they can't do that." Carolina sat up, swinging her feet off the edge of the bed, then caught herself as dizziness swept over her. "We've got to stop them."

"I'm afraid that even Rocket Rogan can't stop them."

"'Rocket Rogan'?"

"That's what they used to call him when he played for the Georgia Bulldogs and ran all over the defense."

"Rogan played ball?"

"Rogan played hardball, even then. But this time I'm afraid he's met his match."

"But—it just isn't fair. The *Scarlet Butterfly* belongs to Rogan. They have to believe that."

"Knowing Sean, if there was a way, he'd have found it. I suppose you know how tunnel-visioned he is. If he wants a thing, he gets it, no matter the expense."

There was bitterness in Ryan Rogan's voice, the same kind of rapier sharpness that she'd heard in Sean's. *Sean.* She'd never thought of him as anything but Rogan. *Rogan*, special, apart from all others, captain of his ship.

But there were other Rogans. And this one was a doctor who'd likely saved her life, and she hadn't even expressed her appreciation. "Thank you for taking care of me, Dr. Rogan," Carolina said, glancing down at the hospital gown she was wearing. "But I have to get back to the *Butterfly*. Where are my clothes?"

"I'm afraid that Rogan brought you here in a sheet. But I'll have my nurse pick up something for you at lunch."

Ryan walked over to the bed and began to check her vital signs. "Whatever possessed you to go without your medication? That was very dangerous. You must have known that something like this would happen."

"My doctor warned me. I didn't think it would happen so fast. And I didn't want to leave him. He's so alone."

Ryan gave a harsh laugh. "Sean? If he's alone, it's because he wants to be. He turned his back on his family—on me especially."

"Why, Ryan? I heard you two talking. I don't have any brothers and sisters, but if I did, I couldn't imagine turning my back on them."

"It's a long story, and one I think you'd best get from him. I guess I ought to thank you for forcing him to come back here, to ask me for help. For the first time in years, we talked. I don't know what will come of it, but at least it's a beginning."

"You seem to be a nice man, Ryan. So is Rogan—Sean. I think it's very hard for him to let himself care."

"He cares about you. You're the first—since Beth."

"'Beth'? Who is Beth?"

"Beth was our sister. Sean loved her very much. Until now, she might be the only person he ever loved unconditionally."

"What happened to Beth?"

"She died. Sean blames me for her death."

Carolina couldn't even think of another question. Sean believed his own brother killed his sister? No wonder he'd become a recluse, closing himself away from the world. No wonder he chose to spend his time with a boat rather than with his family. He probably figured that at least the boat wouldn't betray him.

She realized that Ryan was waiting for some comment. "And are you to blame?"

"No, and even if I was, I've tried to make up for it by establishing a free drug clinic to help others who get on drugs and can't stop. He knew she was experimenting with drugs. So did I. We got them from a friend of mine. In the end I didn't know how bad she was."

Ryan's eyes narrowed in pain, but he didn't try to absolve himself. This kind man kill someone? Carolina's mind refused to accept that, just as it refused to accept the idea that Rogan was some rocket man who intentionally ran roughshod over his family. Whatever he'd done, he'd done in the name of love, just as her father had.

"When is he coming back?"

"I don't think he is. He would never have come this time, except for you. Sean doesn't break his word—ever. And he swore he'd never speak to me again. I'm not sure what was worse for him, your condition or having to go back on his word."

Carolina felt her spirits fall. He'd gone. And he wasn't coming back. What they'd shared hadn't meant anything to Rogan. She was the one who'd fallen in love, who'd gambled that if she stayed with him, he'd see that he cared too.

But he did. Damn him, she knew he did. Otherwise why would he have broken his vow and asked his brother for help? Ryan was wrong. Families were dysfunctional. Certainly her own had been, but family was still family. In spite of his high-handed ways, her father had done only what he'd considered best for her mother, and for herself—just as Rogan had done.

But three days later Rogan still hadn't returned. Ida came by for a visit and to report that the state authorities had booked rooms at her inn for the following week.

Carolina made up her mind. If there was a way to save the *Scarlet Butterfly*, there was only one person who could find it.

She went to the phone and dialed her father's number.

There were times when Jacob wasn't working on the house, or stocking it with supplies, and Carrie would get him to tell her stories about his travels. The one she liked best was the legend of the scarlet butterfly.

Rogan turned the page eagerly. At last he was about to learn about the schooner's name. Carolina would be excited. For a moment he almost called out her name, a thing he'd done without thinking so many times in the last week.

Rogan let out a deep, painful breath. He'd never expected to miss her. He'd never realized that he could share so much, simple things that didn't mean anything. He remembered how fascinated she was with the Spanish moss, the birds, the plop of a fat frog when he jumped into the water. For a woman who'd always had the best, she'd been as excited over learning to fry catfish as she might have been over eating in the finest restaurant.

But Carolina was gone. She'd almost died because he'd been so involved in preserving his solitude that he hadn't paid attention to her condition. If it hadn't been for Jacob, she would have. Rogan hadn't wanted to admit it, but he'd seen the captain. Not once, but several times since he'd returned, the ghostly figure had appeared at his side with a questioning expression on his face.

Finally Rogan had said in exasperation, "The girl's fine. Go back to wherever you came from and quit hovering around. I don't believe in ghosts. Why are you here?"

"I believe I'm here to fulfill a promise to take care of Carolina and her child."

"Well, she doesn't need you. I don't need you," Rogan snapped, as the apparition faded away. Rogan swore. "Now I'm the one talking to a ghost!"

Rogan turned back to the diary. Clearly Carrie and Jacob were waltzing around the growing sexual attraction between them. What wasn't clear was the child. If Carrie wasn't carrying Jacob's child, whose was it? And if Jacob had taken her away, was it because he was in love with her, or because she'd tricked him? Rogan pushed away one final thought of Carolina and began to read.

Jacob says that there was an island in the Pacific on which beautiful scarlet butterflies came to lay their eggs in the only place in the world where they could reproduce, a special place near the top of a volcano. The volcano had been silent for many, many years. But suddenly it came to life again, spitting molten lava high into the air. Finally it spilled over, destroying the butterfly's special place and rolling toward the sea, killing everything in its path. For months the island people prayed to the goddess who lived inside the angry mountain—to no avail.

Finally the high priestess and guardian of the sacred mountain told the people that the only way to appease the goddess was by sacrifice. They must give up the most rare and beautiful thing on the island.

Animals, pearls, and finally a maiden were sacrificed. But the eruptions continued. Finally a little boy trudged to the top of the mountain and released his greatest treasure, a scarlet butterfly he'd captured and kept in a cage. The rumbling stopped and the mountain grew calm. The people were very happy. Only the boy was sad because the butterfly was the last of the rare creatures. They were never seen again.

Carolina must have cried as she wrote, for there were splotches on the paper. Later, according to the journal, Jacob announced he was going to join in the coming war and began to change the colors and markings on his schooner. He asked Carrie to give the schooner a new name.

"The Scarlet Butterfly," she'd answered. *"Because it will always protect you."* And Jacob had begun carving a new figurehead for his ship, a butterfly.

"Jacob, you were a fool," Rogan thought aloud. "The woman was obviously crazy about you, and you're about to go off and leave her to fight a war in which everyone lost. Why didn't you just stay here and nobody would have ever known?"

"Lord help me. I wish I had."

This time Jacob's voice didn't come as a surprise. And Rogan knew that, like Jacob, his life had been changed too. Where he'd once been content to fish and swim alone, to listen to music and read books, now he missed sharing those simple pleasures with someone—with Carolina. He'd called Ryan once, just to make certain that she'd responded to treatment, but he'd refused to talk to her.

He refused Ryan's request to come back for a simple visit, as well as his invitation to the local Rockfish Festival. He couldn't imagine why Ryan would ever expect him to face a crowd, even if he was lonely.

Carolina would be gone, and Ida and Harry weren't exactly the kind of company he'd want, even if he were going to the festival—which he wasn't. The only reason to go into town was to visit the market and pick up the sails for the *Butterfly*. He wouldn't stop by Ryan's office. Ryan wouldn't expect him to come. Carolina wouldn't be there.

Ten

Rogan drove toward town. For the last three days he'd studied his alternatives for saving the schooner. Legally, he had none. Morally, he had none. He was going to lose her, and there wasn't a damned thing he could do about it.

Losing the company had been hard. Losing the *Butterfly* would be worse. Sometime during the last few weeks the schooner and Carolina had become entwined symbolically in his mind, and he couldn't separate the two. A once-proud ship, broken and discarded, had been brought back to life. Carolina, equally damaged, would survive, but would she be broken? He drove down the main street toward the courthouse.

What the hell difference did it make? He'd pick up the sails and hand them over to the state. And he'd let the state figure out how to get the *Butterfly* to the wharf. It would be their problem. Good riddance.

The streets of St. Marys were teeming with people.

Rogan looked around and cursed. No parking places. By the time he finally found a space and ran into the office of the state court judge, Rogan was late. He was stopped short by the man sitting at his attorney's table—Angus Evans. What was he doing there?

Then he knew. Carolina had called her father—to help him.

"Well, Rogan, we wondered if you were going to join us." The judge frowned, and made it clear with his eyes that Rogan had best just sit down without causing any further delay.

"Your honor," Rogan began.

"Sit, Rogan. Your attorney, Mr. Evans, has already pled your case—very eloquently, I might add. I am inclined to accept his suggestion for study."

"But, Your Honor," the state's representative stood and protested, "we've never made a boat a part of the national registry of historical homesites. That regulation has only applied to houses."

"You're out of order, sir. Your objection has already been noted. If the object of the law is to designate something an historic landmark in order to protect it for the people to see and enjoy, I can see no reason that a ship on which an individual lives can't be declared one. If Mr. Rogan is willing to allow the public to view the *Scarlet Butterfly* on some kind of reasonable schedule and maintain the vessel without assistance from the historical funds, it seems to me that might solve all our problems."

Rogan, still standing in the aisle, came forward. "But, Your Honor, I would never allow—"

"Of course you would, Rogan." Carolina rose from her seat in the rear and came to take Sean's hand

and stand beside him. "It's what Jacob and Carrie would have wanted. Don't you see?"

All he could see was Carolina, looking up at him with her eyes shining and her lips parted in a happy smile.

"You asked for your father's help?"

"You asked for your brother's, after you vowed never to talk to him again."

"But you wanted to escape your father's control."

"I was wrong. He really only wanted to care for me, just as you tried to care for your family. You thought your family let you down. You were wrong, weren't you."

"Maybe I was," he admitted. "I've been thinking about that, Carrie—and about you."

"Ahem! Mr. Rogan, if you two would like to continue this conversation outside my courtroom, I'll discuss this further with Mr. Evans and the state attorney. Oh, and Mr. Rogan—if you appear in my court again, get a haircut. You look like a river pirate."

They were walking along the river, dodging the tourists, holding hands.

"I'm going to stay here, in St. Marys, Rogan. I don't intend to let you rule my life, but I will share the making of our decisions. Ryan says that I probably can't give you children, so I won't expect you to marry me. I'll just be here for you as long or as often as you need me."

Rogan bit back a smile.

"Very generous of you, Goldilocks, but there are certain decisions I've always made, and that I'll continue to make—among them, who shares my bed, and under what conditions."

"I see. Then I guess I'd better go." She stopped and turned back toward the crowds, hoping she could hide herself before Rogan saw the tears that threatened to spill over at any minute.

"You are not going anywhere, Carolina Evans. You started all this, and you're going to see it through. You have to finish the portrait, and I found something in the house—one of Carrie's journals."

Carolina whirled back around and flung her arms around Rogan's neck. "You did? What did it say? What—How—?"

"I don't know. I only read the beginning. I couldn't go on, not without you. It was your dream, Carolina. You've got to be the one to finish it."

"My 'dream'?"

"Our dream," he admitted in a low voice as he felt that special calm steal over him. Her eyes held such certainty. Her lips were inviting—no, *asking* him to take them. He'd been so sure that he knew what was best. He'd been wrong. Carolina knew all along. She'd made herself a part of his life. Everything he'd tried to close out, she'd put back: being needed, wanting, and having his needs answered.

His hands went to her shoulders, holding her still as he tried to stop his own tremors. She'd stormed into his world and made him care again. "Ah, Carolina, darling, you understood all along. I didn't think I could ever love anybody again, but I do love you. I'll try very hard to make you happy."

He'd try to make her happy. Carolina sighed in contentment. Nobody had ever told her that before. Do what was best for her, look after her—but make her *happy*? And she knew that he meant it. She'd trusted him from the beginning. And when his lips came down on hers, she surrendered herself to him completely.

"Whoee-eee, man! Way to go," he heard a stranger's voice cry out.

Rogan raised his head. He was practically making love to Carolina in the middle of the wharf, in the middle of the annual Rock Fish Festival. A more public display couldn't have been arranged. And for once he didn't care. He was with his girl, the woman he intended to marry.

"Let's get out of here," he said, taking her by the hand and rushing her back to his truck.

"Where are we going?"

"Home. Back to the *Butterfly*, before she disappears."

"Why would she disappear?"

"The original scarlet butterflies became extinct hundreds of years ago, Carrie. The last one was sacrificed to save an island. I think our *Butterfly* might have accomplished the same thing."

"I don't understand," Carolina said as Rogan lifted her into the seat and crawled in behind her.

"Come here, woman." He kissed her again, quick and hard, then started the engine. At least one good thing had come from his having had to park so far away from the courthouse: He could avoid the traffic. In no time they had reached the schooner. Rogan climbed out of the truck, took Carrie in his arms, and kissed her again.

"Awwwk! Pretty Carrie. Pretty Carrie's home!"

Inside the cabin Carolina pulled away, her face flushed, her heart pounding wildly. "Am I, Rogan?"

"You certainly are!" Rogan let Carolina's feet slide to the floor, his hands slowly unbuttoning and removing her clothes. "You've gained weight," he said, leaning down and kissing one nipple and then the other before pushing her back on the bed.

There was a smile on his face as he unbuttoned and removed his own clothes. She could feel the restraint in him, restraint and something else. Then, as he knelt down, cupping her breasts with his hands, she saw it—the shadow behind in the passageway.

Jacob. She knew and understood. She wondered why she didn't feel embarrassed at being watched, but she didn't. When Rogan pressed her against the bed and moved over her, she noticed the shadow moving closer. As if she were watching Rogan in one of those cut-glass windows, she could see two of him—her glorious rascal, nude and announcing his desire with his body, and the shadow of the man who'd been the catalyst for their finding each other.

Suddenly the cabin was filled with the scent of tobacco and wildflowers.

"Rogan," she whispered. But the name that echoed in the silence was "*Jacob.*"

"*Yes, Carrie, I love you. I'll never leave you again. My vow is fulfilled.*"

As Carolina watched, Jacob gave her a smile, turned, and walked away, joining hands with the young woman standing in the shadows at the top of the stairs.

"*You know they're going to rebuild our house,*" Jacob said.

"*I know,*" the woman answered.

"*Can we share our house with them?*" Jacob asked.

"I think so. They've brought the Butterfly *back to you."*

In the cabin below Rogan deepened his kisses, entering Carolina's body with such wonder and delight that she knew without a doubt that she was with the man she loved.

Gone were those black, vacant eyes filled with coldness. Rogan moved slowly, leaning back so that he could explore her face, her neck, and her lips with his tongue, loving her as if for the first time.

And his touch fanned the flame that danced just beneath her skin. His hands kneaded her bare skin with a feverish rhythm. Carolina felt heat in every part of her body. Her hands sought the feel of his beautiful shaped shoulders, the powerful muscles in his back, his smooth buttocks.

Then she sensed it, the beginning of the eruption. Her body buckled and thrashed in its urgency, and she knew that Rogan was feeling the same searing need for release.

He was taking deep, slow breaths, plunging inside her and pulling out again in an agonizing motion, holding as long as he could before the tremors finally burst loose, exploding in spasms of fire that shook the bed with their magnitude.

Later, when Carolina was lying in his arms, content and half-asleep, Rogan told her the legend of the scarlet butterfly and how their ship had gotten its name, about how symbolic it was that its modern-day loss had brought them together.

"Why did you call your father, Carolina?"

"Because if anyone could save the schooner, he could."

"You're right." Rogan planted a kiss on the top of

her head. "I still can't believe it. I'd studied and considered every possible alternative for weeks and it
never occurred to me that I could have it declared a
house to be placed on the registry of homes."

"I told you my father got what he wanted."

"You're right about the similarity," Rogan said,
"because I got what I wanted too. Are you sure you're
all right, darling?"

"I'm very much all right. If I were any more all
right, I'd probably soar right off this bed and take the
Butterfly with me, without her sails." She pressed
her face against his chest. She wanted to talk about
the depth of her feelings, but she didn't know how.

"But are you sure, Carolina, about being here with
me? I'll always be pretty much of a loner, even if I do
change. I don't know much about loving."

"You've never been in love before?"

"No, I don't think I have. Every time I ever cared
about something, I lost it."

Carolina hesitated. "You mean like Beth?"

"Beth? Ryan told you about Beth?"

"No, he only told me that you cared about her and
that she died. He didn't tell me how."

"All right. You should know it all. Beth was my
youngest sister. She was the light of my life—full of
fun, bright. Then she got into drugs, through a
friend of Ryan's. Ryan never really knew how bad
she was. He thought he could help her, so he and the
family kept it from me."

Carolina felt the tension sweep over Rogan. She
reached for his hand and pulled it to her lips. "And
she died?"

"Yes. I know now that it wasn't Ryan's fault. I
thought that if he'd told me, I could have stopped

her, just like I'd fixed the business problems. To me, if there was a problem, there was a solution. It was that simple.

"The family took Ryan's side, defending him when I accused him of not doing enough. After that Ryan went to medical school, and I became obsessed with proving that I was some superman who could do what my family couldn't. If I could do just a little more, I figured, the pain would be over."

"When I was a little girl I used to blame my father for my mother's drinking. If he'd be kinder to her, more caring, she'd stop. But there was some dark part of her that he couldn't fix. All he could do was look after her, and he did."

"That's what I did too. And that only made Beth's problem worse. She didn't want to let me down, so she denied there was a problem. And because I loved her, I believed her."

"We can't go on blaming ourselves, Rogan. We can't change the past. All we can do now is take care of each other." She ran her toes along his inner thigh suggestively. "And speaking of being taken care of . . ."

It was the next day before Rogan retrieved Carrie's diary and left Carolina to read it undisturbed. When she reached the explanation of the butterfly, she read to the bottom of the entry and waited for Rogan to complete his swim and climb back on board.

"Come and join me in the hammock," she said, drawing to her feet. "I've wanted to share it with you since that first night."

Rogan stood in the sunlight, lifting his face to the

heat. Soon it would be too cool, even here, to swim nude and depend on the sun's rays to dry off. Soon he'd have to find a better place for the woman he already considered himself married to.

"Why didn't *you* join *me* in the hammock?"

"I was afraid of what you might say."

He took her hand and drew her close. "Carolina, darling, I have my doubts that I'd have done any talking at all."

Later, when they finally did collapse in the hammock, determined to read the remainder of the diary, they were surprised to find a strange handwriting.

I should never have left her. But I was consumed with guilt over lying with her, not once but over and over again, like some wild animal in heat. I could not get enough of her sweet body. It mattered not that another man had had her first, that she'd delivered a daughter who wasn't mine. I loved the child as if it were. No, it was worse. For now I'd gotten her with child, my child, and I had to leave. The war was in full force now, and I could no longer hide away on the river, turning my back on the great need for medicine and supplies. I was afraid for our child and what our loving might do to it, but she said I was not to fear, the babe's coming was still weeks away. And I lay with her one last time. She was mine now, and Lord help me, I loved her.

But at last I had to go. I didn't want to leave her, and I know now that she deliberately sent me away. And I, who offered my services so gallantly to serve the South, only made one quick little voyage to the port of Orleans and back, bringing in not medicine and food supplies, but weapons with which to hurt and kill.

I might still have fulfilled my mission but for the

Union boat that intercepted me. Once the ship drew close I recognized its captain, Carrie's father. I couldn't return fire. I couldn't even face him. Rather, I turned and sailed my schooner home, back up the St. Marys to Carrie.

I was too late. I'd rashly promised to take care of Carrie and her babe. But she'd already been in labor for days. Finally she was delivered of a child, a poor pitiful little male child who died, along with my darling Carrie. I think this must be a punishment for my sins. I could not fulfill my promise, Carrie, not in this lifetime, but I vow that I will try. At my feet, as I write, is your daughter, the child with those silver-blue eyes.

Eyes that ask.

Eyes that must be answered.

I promise you once, Carrie. I now promise you again.

Carolina turned the page. It was blank. She raised her gaze to Rogan's. "There were two children."

"Yes. Your great-great-great-great-great-great-great-grandmother, Carrie's daughter. And Jacob's son."

"Oh, Rogan. The baby died. Does that mean that you're not Jacob's descendant?"

"We may never know, darling. Jacob could have had many wives and many children, or his family might have come from Charleston to claim his land. What happened over a hundred years ago has nothing to do with us."

Carolina closed the book and laid it on the deck beside them, then turned back to claim her spot in Rogan's arms. "I think it does," she said with a sigh of satisfaction. "I don't know what Carrie expected when she ran away with Jacob, but they're together now. And this Carolina didn't know exactly what she wanted, either, until she found it."

The boat shifted and a faint whiff of tobacco ribboned the air where the two lovers lay.

"Do you think we're alone, Carolina?"

"No, I think Jacob and Carrie will always be with us. Do you mind?"

He looked down at her face, now flushed with pleasure. "Not a bit," he said, and kissed her.

Later, as they sat on deck, Rogan asked a question that surprised even himself. "How would you feel about your husband smoking a pipe?"

"I'd think one pipe smoker in the Rogan family is enough," she answered with a twinkle in her eye.

The wedding was performed in the spring in the parlor of Ridgeway Inn. Angus Evans gave the bride away. Ryan Rogan was the best man, and Ida and Harry acted as witnesses. Afterward the entire town, including the rest of the Rogan family, came down to the docks to watch the *Scarlet Butterfly* make its maiden voyage south to a Caribbean island. The schooner, it had been decided, would eventually be moored at the wharf where the St. Marys River met the Atlantic Ocean, and would be open year-round for all the world to see.

Sean and Carolina were almost finished restoring their house on the St. Marys River. And Carolina's portrait of the ship was finished and ready to hang over the mantel.

And if an observer looked real close at the painting and had a bit of imagination, it was sometimes possible to see the shadowy figure of the ship's captain pacing the deck. Carolina just laughed when guests asked. She didn't think it at all odd that the figure seemed to be in different places depending on who was watching.

After all, Jacob had always had a mind of his own, and like Carrie, Carolina wouldn't have changed him if she could have.

Epilogue

"What do you mean you might lose her? Ryan, you've delivered hundreds of babies."

"Sean, I warned you, and I warned Carolina, that getting pregnant was a risk, that she might not be able to carry a child. I don't know why you let it happen."

"Carolina wanted a child so badly, Ryan. I never intended for this to happen. But when it did, I couldn't refuse her. Neither could you. It's been three years, Ryan. Surely you doctors have learned something new. Please, Ryan, you have to do something. Having a baby doesn't kill women, not in today's world. There are modern miracles. Can't we call in somebody?"

Ryan sighed. They'd had this conversation almost daily since he'd learned that Carolina was pregnant. "It wouldn't do any good. I'm scheduling a c-section. The baby is showing signs of distress, and I don't like Carolina's blood pressure."

"I'll call Angus," Sean said, his voice low and wavery. "He ought to know."

"You do that, and when you get back, just wait here in Carrie's room. Call the nurse if you need her. I'll get set up."

Angus said he'd come immediately. Sean thought a moment, then called his mother. They might never be close, but they were finding their way back to each other, thanks to Carrie's insisting that their baby should have a grandmother.

Back in Carrie's room, Sean sat on the chair beside her bed and took her hand. She was pale, very pale, as pale as she had been that first day he'd found her in his bed on board the *Butterfly*.

So much had happened since then. He'd learned how to love and how to be loved. His entire life had changed so much that he hardly remembered a time when Carolina hadn't been the center of it. And she'd been happy too. Until he'd made her pregnant, she'd been as bright and warm as the sunlight that seemed to follow her.

Now she was sedated.

Suddenly she opened her eyes.

"Hi, Captain."

"Hi, Sleeping Beauty. You know, I called you Goldilocks the first time I saw you because of your haircut, but I really thought you were waiting for your prince to kiss you awake."

"I still am," she whispered.

He kissed her gently. "Don't worry, darling Carolina. I'll take care of you and our baby. I promise."

"I know," she said, "you both will."

As Ryan and the nurse wheeled Carolina away, Rogan sat in the darkness. He reached for a pipe, then laughed. A thousand times he'd thought about buying a pipe, but he'd never done it.

In the lobby he found a shop that sold cigarettes, pipes, and tobacco. He picked out a fine-looking carved pipe with a curved handle, along with a pouch of tobacco, and paid the clerk.

"You know, you can't smoke that in the hospital," she reminded him. "But there's a solarium outside the second-floor waiting room that you can use."

"I don't need to smoke it," he said, patting his jacket pocket. "I just needed to have it."

Back in the room, he waited. After what seemed like hours the door opened and Carrie's bed was rolled back inside. She was still half-asleep, but she was all right.

"The baby?" Rogan whispered to his brother, who had come in behind her.

"The baby's going to be fine," Ryan answered, adding, "No thanks to you."

"To me?"

"You didn't have to give her a linebacker. She's much too small to carry such a child."

For the rest of the night Rogan slept with his head on her bed. In the morning the nurse brought their child, laid it in its mother's arms, and left the room.

"Come and look, Rogan. We have a beautiful son."

Rogan watched as the child stared at his father for a moment, then grasped his mother's nipple with relish. "He has eyes like his mother, silver-blue eyes," Rogan said, with a catch of wonder in his throat.

"Yes, but he has his father's greedy touch."

"What will we call him?" Rogan asked.

"I thought, if you approve, we'd call him Jacob."

"Jacob is a fine name."

They watched the child nurse.

"Rogan, have you taken up smoking that pipe I see in your pocket?"

"No, why?"

"Then he's here. I smell pipe tobacco."

"So do I. I've smelled it most of the night. I thought it might be because of the dampness, from the rain."

"It's raining? I can't see it, Rogan. Will you open the window?"

It seemed to be stopping. Rogan tugged until he managed to raise the window a few inches. The smell of the sea rushed in, the sea and summer flowers. And then, hovering in the open space, there appeared a flash of red.

"Look, Rogan."

The red, lacy butterfly fluttered there for a moment, then dipped its wings and flew away.

"A scarlet butterfly," Carolina whispered. "It's a miracle. Thank you, Jacob."

The child opened his eyes and smiled. Outside the rain stopped and the sun came out.

In the harbor beyond, the boats floated like colored leaves on the water. Back in the saltwater lake the silt shifted, releasing its hold on the buried wooden figure. Gracefully it bobbed to the surface and floated by the dock. Aged and weathered, the figurehead moved back and forth, washing the mud from its graceful wings.

Mystically, it righted itself, planting its base in the mud by the shore. And then, as the rays of the sun pierced the foliage overhead, a tiny red butterfly flitted through the air and settled on the tip of the wooden wing.

Like a verbal sigh, the sound of the wind ribboned across the air and disappeared into the woods.

"*What do you think, lass?*"

"*A scarlet butterfly. Carolina has her son, and she's fine. I think it's time we went back to the ship, Jacob. They don't need us anymore.*"

The butterfly rested in her special chosen spot for a very long time; then, as if weary beyond belief, she fluttered her wings and flew away, leaving behind her the promise of new life to come.

Of promises fulfilled.

Of dreams come true.

THE EDITOR'S CORNER

Next month's lineup sizzles with BAD BOYS, heroes who are too hot to handle but too sinful to resist. In six marvelous romances, you'll be held spellbound by these men's deliciously wicked ways and daring promises of passion. Whether they're high-powered attorneys, brash jet jockeys, or modern-day pirates, BAD BOYS are masters of seduction who never settle for anything less than what they want. And the heroines learn that surrender comes all too easily when the loving is all too good. . . .

Fighter pilot Devlin MacKenzie in **MIDNIGHT STORM** by Laura Taylor, LOVESWEPT #576, is the first of our BAD BOYS. He and David Winslow, the hero of DESERT ROSE, LOVESWEPT #555, flew together on a mission that ended in a horrible crash, and now Devlin has come to Jessica Cleary's inn to recuperate. She broke their engagement years before, afraid to love a man who lives dangerously, but the rugged warrior changes her mind in a scorchingly sensual courtship. Laura turns up the heat in this riveting romance.

SHAMELESS, LOVESWEPT #577, by Glenna McReynolds, is the way Colt Haines broke Sarah Brooks's heart by leaving town without a word after the night she'd joyfully given him her innocence. Ten years later a tragedy brings him back to Rock Creek, Wyoming. He vows not to stay, but with one look at the woman she's become, he's determined to make her understand why he'd gone—and to finally make her his. Ablaze with the intensity of Glenna's writing, **SHAMELESS** is a captivating love story.

Cutter Beaumont *is* an **ISLAND ROGUE**, LOVESWEPT #578, by Charlotte Hughes, and he's also the mayor, sheriff, and owner of the Last Chance Saloon. Ellie Parks isn't interested though. She's come to the South Carolina island looking for a peaceful place to silence the demons that haunt her dreams—and instead she finds a handsome rake who wants to keep her up nights. Charlotte masterfully resolves this trouble in paradise with a series of events that will make you laugh and cry.

Jake Madison is nothing but **BAD COMPANY** for Nila Shepherd in Theresa Gladden's new LOVESWEPT, #579. When his sensual gaze spots her across the casino, Jake knows he must possess the temptress in the come-and-get-me dress. Nila has always wanted to walk on the wild side, but the fierce desire Jake awakens in her has her running for cover. Still, there's no hiding from this man who makes it his mission to fulfill her fantasies. Theresa just keeps coming up with terrific romances, and aren't we lucky?

Our next LOVESWEPT, #580 by Olivia Rupprecht, has one of the best titles ever—**HURTS SO GOOD**. And legendary musician Neil Grey certainly knows about hurting; that's why he dropped out of the rat race and now plays only in his New Orleans bar. Journalist Andrea Post would try just about anything to uncover his mystery, to write the story no one ever had, but the moment he calls her *"chère,"* he steals her heart. Another memorable winner from Olivia!

Suzanne Forster's stunning contribution to the BAD BOYS month is **NIGHT OF THE PANTHER**, LOVESWEPT #581. Johnny Starhawk is a celebrated lawyer whose killer instincts and Irish-Apache heritage have made him a star, but he's never forgotten the woman who'd betrayed him. And now, when Honor Bartholomew is forced to seek his help, will he give in to his need for revenge . . . or his love for the only woman he's ever wanted? This romance of smoldering anger and dangerous desire is a tour de force from Suzanne.

On sale this month from FANFARE are four terrific novels. **DIVINE EVIL** is the most chilling romantic suspense novel yet from best-selling author Nora Roberts. When successful sculptor Clare Kimball returns to her hometown, she discovers that there's a high price to pay for digging up the secrets of the past. But she finds an ally in the local sheriff, and together they confront an evil all the more terrifying because those who practice it believe it is divine.

HAVING IT ALL by critically acclaimed author Maeve Haran is a tender, funny, and revealing novel about a woman who does have it all—a glittering career, an exciting husband, and two adorable children. But she tires of pretending she's superwoman, and her search for a different kind of happiness and success shocks the family and friends she loves.

With **HIGHLAND FLAME**, Stephanie Bartlett brings back the beloved heroine of HIGHLAND REBEL. In this new novel, Catriona Galbraid and her husband, Ian, depart Scotland's Isle of Skye after they're victorious in their fight for justice for the crofters. But when a tragedy leaves Cat a widow, she's thrust into a new struggle—and into the arms of a new love.

Talented Virginia Lynn creates an entertaining variation on the taming-of-the-shrew theme with **LYON'S PRIZE**. In medieval England the Saxon beauty Brenna of Marwald is forced to marry Rye de Lyon, the Norman knight known as the Black Lion. She vows that he will never have her love, but he captures her heart with passion.

Sharon and Tom Curtis are among the most talented authors of romantic fiction, and you wouldn't want to miss this chance to pick up a copy of their novel **THE GOLDEN TOUCH**, which LaVyrle Spencer has praised as being "pure pleasure!" This beautifully written romance has two worlds colliding when an internationally famous pop idol moves into the life of a small-town teacher.

The Delaneys are coming! Once again Kay Hooper, Iris Johansen, and Fayrene Preston have collaborated to bring you a sparkling addition to this remarkable family's saga. Look for **THE DELANEY CHRISTMAS CAROL**— available soon from FANFARE.

Happy reading!

With best wishes,

Nita Taublib

Nita Taublib
Associate Publisher
LOVESWEPT and FANFARE

OFFICIAL RULES TO WINNERS CLASSIC SWEEPSTAKES

No Purchase necessary. To enter the sweepstakes follow instructions found elsewhere in this offer. You can also enter the sweepstakes by hand printing your name, address, city, state and zip code on a 3" x 5" piece of paper and mailing it to: Winners Classic Sweepstakes, P.O. Box 785, Gibbstown, NJ 08027. Mail each entry separately. Sweepstakes begins 12/1/91. Entries must be received by 6/1/93. Some presentations of this sweepstakes may feature a deadline for the Early Bird prize. If the offer you receive does, then to be eligible for the Early Bird prize your entry must be received according to the Early Bird date specified. Not responsible for lost, late, damaged, misdirected, illegible or postage due mail. Mechanically reproduced entries are not eligible. All entries become property of the sponsor and will not be returned.

Prize Selection/Validations: Winners will be selected in random drawings on or about 7/30/93, by VENTURA ASSOCIATES, INC., an independent judging organization whose decisions are final. Odds of winning are determined by total number of entries received. Circulation of this sweepstakes is estimated not to exceed 200 million. Entrants need not be present to win. All prizes are guaranteed to be awarded and delivered to winners. Winners will be notified by mail and may be required to complete an affidavit of eligibility and release of liability which must be returned within 14 days of date of notification or alternate winners will be selected. Any guest of a trip winner will also be required to execute a release of liability. Any prize notification letter or any prize returned to a participating sponsor, Bantam Doubleday Dell Publishing Group, Inc., its participating divisions or subsidiaries, or VENTURA ASSOCIATES, INC. as undeliverable will be awarded to an alternate winner. Prizes are not transferable. No multiple prize winners except as may be necessary due to unavailability, in which case a prize of equal or greater value will be awarded. Prizes will be awarded approximately 90 days after the drawing. All taxes, automobile license and registration fees, if applicable, are the sole responsibility of the winners. Entry constitutes permission (except where prohibited) to use winners' names and likenesses for publicity purposes without further or other compensation.

Participation: This sweepstakes is open to residents of the United States and Canada, except for the province of Quebec. This sweepstakes is sponsored by Bantam Doubleday Dell Publishing Group, Inc. (BDD), 666 Fifth Avenue, New York, NY 10103. Versions of this sweepstakes with different graphics will be offered in conjunction with various solicitations or promotions by different subsidiaries and divisions of BDD. Employees and their families of BDD, its division, subsidiaries, advertising agencies, and VENTURA ASSOCIATES, INC., are not eligible.

Canadian residents, in order to win, must first correctly answer a time limited arithmetical skill testing question. Void in Quebec and wherever prohibited or restricted by law. Subject to all federal, state, local and provincial laws and regulations.

Prizes: The following values for prizes are determined by the manufacturers' suggested retail prices or by what these items are currently known to be selling for at the time this offer was published. Approximate retail values include handling and delivery of prizes. Estimated maximum retail value of prizes: 1 Grand Prize ($27,500 if merchandise or $25,000 Cash); 1 First Prize ($3,000); 5 Second Prizes ($400 each); 35 Third Prizes ($100 each); 1,000 Fourth Prizes ($9.00 each) ; 1 Early Bird Prize ($5,000); Total approximate maximum retail value is $50,000. Winners will have the option of selecting any prize offered at level won. Automobile winner must have a valid driver's license at the time the car is awarded. Trips are subject to space and departure availability. Certain black-out dates may apply. Travel must be completed within one year from the time the prize is awarded. Minors must be accompanied by an adult. Prizes won by minors will be awarded in the name of parent or legal guardian.

For a list of Major Prize Winners (available after 7/30/93): send a self-addressed, stamped envelope entirely separate from your entry to: Winners Classic Sweepstakes Winners, P.O. Box 825, Gibbstown, NJ 08027. Requests must be received by 6/1/93. DO NOT SEND ANY OTHER CORRESPONDENCE TO THIS P.O. BOX.

SWP 9/92

Q-Ville Service

(212) 379-6761

The Delaney Dynasty lives on in

The Delaney
Christmas Carol

by Kay Hooper, Iris Johansen, &
Fayrene Preston

Three of romantic fiction's best-loved authors present the changing face of Christmas spirit—past, present, and future—as they tell the story of three generations of Delaneys in love.

CHRISTMAS PAST by Iris Johansen

From the moment he first laid eyes on her, Kevin Delaney felt a curious attraction for the ragclad Gypsy beauty rummaging through the attic of his ranch at Killara. He didn't believe for a moment her talk of magic mirrors and second-sight, but something about Zara St. Cloud stirred his blood. Now, as Christmas draws near, a touch leads to a kiss and a gift of burning passion.

CHRISTMAS PRESENT by Fayrene Preston

Bria Delaney had been looking for Christmas ornaments in her mother's attic, when she saw him in the mirror for the first time—a stunningly handsome man with sky-blue eyes and red-gold hair. She had almost convinced herself he was only a dream when Kells Braxton arrived at Killara and led them both to a holiday wonderland of sensuous pleasure.

CHRISTMAS FUTURE by Kay Hooper

As the last of the Delaney men, Brett returned to Killara this Christmastime only to find it in the capable hands of his father's young and beautiful widow. Yet the closer he got to Cassie, the more Brett realized that the embers of their old love still burned and that all it would take was a look, a kiss, a caress, to turn their dormant passion into an inferno.

The best in Women's Fiction from Bantam FANFARE.
On sale in November 1992   AN 428 9/92